It looked as if someone had spilled red paint.

As she dabbed at the spot, it came up easily. "Is anyone here?" Shona called, feeling a twinge of unease.

The stain looked like blood.

"Dad?" she called more loudly as she rushed through the kitchen. She saw another splotch of red by the stairs.

Following one droplet after another, she climbed to the second floor, where she saw a dark form splayed.

"Dad!" She saw him lying on his back, his arms at his side.

Blood streaked down his face from his nose and caked his thick gray hair. He opened his eyes and tried to speak.

Shona pulled her cell phone from her pocket and called 9-1-1.

"Please hurry," she said to the dispatcher over the telephone. "My father is in bad shape."

As the voice reassured her that help would be there soon, she wanted to scream. Soon might be too late.

Books by Hannah Alexander

Steeple Hill Single Title

*Hideaway
*Safe Haven
*Last Resort
*Fair Warning

*Hideaway

Love Inspired Suspense

*Note of Peril #1
*Under Suspicion #25

HANNAH ALEXANDER

is the pseudonym of husband-and-wife writing team Cheryl and Mel Hodde (pronounced "Hoddee"). When they first met, Mel had just begun his new job as an E.R. doctor in Cheryl's hometown, and Cheryl was working on a novel. Cheryl's matchmaking pastor set them up on an unexpected blind date at a local restaurant. Surprised by the sneak attack, Cheryl blurted the first thing that occurred to her, "You're a doctor? Could you help me paralyze someone?" Mel was shocked. "Only temporarily, of course," she explained when she saw his expression. "And only fictitiously. I'm writing a novel."

They began brainstorming immediately. Eighteen months later they were married, and the novels they set in fictitious Ozark towns began to sell. The first novel of the series, *Hideaway*, published in the Steeple Hill Women's Fiction program, won the prestigious Christy Award for Best Romance in 2004.

HANNAH ALEXANDER

Under Suspicion

Steeple
Hill®

Published by Steeple Hill Books™

STEEPLE HILL BOOKS

Steeple
Hill®

ISBN-13: 978-0-373-87377-7
ISBN-10:   0-373-87377-8

UNDER SUSPICION

Copyright © 2006 by Hannah Alexander

All rights reserved. Except for use in any review, the reproduction
or utilization of this work in whole or in part in any form by any
electronic, mechanical or other means, now known or hereafter
invented, including xerography, photocopying and recording, or in
any information storage or retrieval system, is forbidden without
the written permission of the editorial office, Steeple Hill Books,
233 Broadway, New York, NY 10279 U.S.A.

All characters in this book have no existence outside the imagination of
the author and have no relation whatsoever to anyone bearing the same
name or names. They are not even distantly inspired by any individual
known or unknown to the author, and all incidents are pure invention.

This edition published by arrangement with Steeple Hill Books.

® and TM are trademarks of Steeple Hill Books, used under license.
Trademarks indicated with ® are registered in the United States Patent
and Trademark Office, the Canadian Trade Marks Office and in other
countries.

www.SteepleHill.com

Printed in U.S.A.

Trust in the Lord with all your heart
and do not lean on your own understanding.
In all your ways acknowledge Him,
and He will make your paths straight.
—*Proverbs* 3:5–6

Many thanks to Lorene Cook for living a life of love and giving that constantly inspires us. Thanks to Harry Styron, attorney-at-law, for supplying vital personal and professional information for this story. Thanks, as always, to Joan Marlow Golan and our other wonderful editors for gently helping us bring this story to life. Thanks to Nancy Moser, Till Fell, Colleen and Dave Coble, Stephanie and Dan Higgins, Rene Gutteridge, Judy Miller and Deborah Raney for the great brainstorm session. Thanks to Barbara Warren, Jackie Bolton and Bonnie Schmidt for your valuable input.

ONE

It's time to get a new life.

Shona Tremaine tapped the brake and turned into the curving, tree-lined drive that led to her father's mansion. For now, it was home to her, but a break was coming soon.

She needed to distance herself from the cutting edge of Dad's politics as a state senator in Jefferson City, Missouri. That edge was serrated, and she had allowed it to slice right down the middle of her marriage—and everything else in her life.

Two weeks ago had been the final straw, and her showdown with her father in the Capitol Building had been loud and public. How could she have let that happen? She knew better, but she'd been so furious with Dad for breaking a promise to his constituents that for once she couldn't help herself.

When she and Geoff separated last year, it had made sense to her to move into her old bedroom suite in Dad's massive home. She spent a lot of time in his office in that house, working on his behalf. So now, she was not only grieving the loss of her marriage, but also her home, as well as the increasingly unethical choices Dad had been making lately—of which she saw too much from her front-row seat here at the mansion.

As her father's top aide/personal assistant, Shona topped the senator's short list of confidants, for Kemper MacDonald trusted few people in this town—or even in the whole state of Missouri.

Instead of pulling into the five-car garage in back of the mansion, she parked her white Cadillac Escalade beneath the willow trees in the front drive. She and Dad were to be guests this evening at a dinner hosted by the Citizens for a Drug Free Missouri.

Other guests were members of the Drug Task Force, including State Representative Paul Forester, one of Dad's dearest friends, an old hunting buddy. Paul—who had dropped out of medical school thirty years ago—had a son who had been in a medical residency program with Shona's younger sister Karah Lee. For a while, the two fathers had hoped there might be a romance between their children. It never happened. But to Shona, the Foresters would always be like family.

Also attending was another of Dad's old friends, State Representative Linda Plinkett. Shona suspected her father had been fraternizing with Linda quite often in the past months, until very recently.

Missouri politics was a tight, if often uneasy, community.

Tonight would be interesting, Shona mused, since Dad and Linda had barely spoken to one another in the past two weeks. They'd even been avoiding eye contact when in the same room. In fact, Shona had noticed this sudden coolness soon after her own fight with Dad.

Very curious, indeed.

As Shona stepped from her SUV into the cooling air this Friday evening, mature oaks, maples and majestic broadleaf pines whispered to her on the breeze. May had always been one of her favorite months, and this one promised to be particularly fine. She wished she had time to appreciate it properly.

She ascended the wide steps to the verandah, unable to resist a glance toward the state capitol building to the west, its white dome turning pink-and-gold in the glow of the setting sun. Below, the Missouri River meandered with lazy abandon in its journey toward the Mississippi.

She'd always loved this city. For many years she had loved her job, working with her father and her husband to serve the residents of Missouri.

As time passed, however, she and Geoff had both realized that Dad was losing the ideals with which he had begun his career. His professional ethics had gone the way of his personal morals.

Why should she have been surprised?

Last year was the lowest point, when Geoff gave

Dad a letter of resignation and asked Shona to do the same. She'd felt forced to choose between her husband and her father. And she'd made the wrong choice.

Geoff was strong and confident, needing help from no one. Dad, on the other hand, had always needed her. She'd felt that if anyone could keep her father on solid ethical ground, it would be her.

How wrong could a woman be?

Lately, more and more, she'd been experiencing the sting of loss. Could her relationship with Geoff be rectified before the divorce was final? She had been the one to file in the first place. She'd left Geoff, spurred by her anger at his defection and his ultimatum that she do the same.

Geoff had landed on his feet after resigning as Dad's top aide. With his background and degree in communications, he was now a reporter and anchor for the six-o'clock news on Jefferson City's Channel 6.

Shona seldom missed the news these days, and yet she found it painful to watch. It just made her miss her husband more, and realize her loss more sharply.

Tonight, after the dinner, she would have a talk with Dad about her need to be independent from him. She would officially resign and offer to help him find her replacement, but after that, who knew?

She hated to leave politics altogether, though that was essentially what she would be doing. Dad was the one who had mentored her, grooming her to run for his Senate office when he made his bid for the governorship.

She only knew she needed out before the compromises she made at Dad's behest destroyed the final foundations of her character. Since the fight, she and Dad had barely communicated unless it was about work. Dad didn't seem angry with her, just very preoccupied.

She pressed her electronic key into the plate at the side of the front door and waited for the sequence of numbers to be translated into the main computer that controlled security. The door slid open and she entered, glancing at her watch. There would barely be time to shower, change and slide into the new creation of burgundy silk she had purchased last week for this dinner.

First, she would find Dad and remind him of what he was to wear tonight—the understated dark gray Armani suit, with a fit that hinted at the power behind the facade. Whenever he was in public, he wanted to dress the part, although he had little fashion sense, much like Karah Lee, his younger daughter.

Halfway across the formal dining room en route to the kitchen, Shona spotted something on the floor. It looked as if someone had spilled some of the dark red paint that a crew had been using for a touch-up job on the garage.

She winced at the thought of her father's reaction

when he saw it. Kemper MacDonald had never had a lot of patience with mistakes or messes.

The housekeeper, Mrs. Reynolds, had Friday afternoons off, so Shona didn't call out. She pushed through the swinging doors into the kitchen to get a paper towel to clean the mess.

Her father was probably upstairs in his suite, showering.

She dabbed at the spot. It came up easily. It was obviously fresh. Examining the paper towel more closely, she felt a twinge of unease. She sniffed it. Not paint. Not catsup. Was that a coppery scent?

Don't panic. It's your imagination. Dad has always teased you about your vivid imagination. She tossed the paper towel in the trash as she rushed through the kitchen, suddenly noticing another splotch of red by the back door.

Following one droplet after another, she turned left into Dad's home office. In the dim light of the setting sun, she saw a human form—a man—splayed on the floor, faceup, between a corner of the desk and the French windows. A stain of blood fanned out from beneath his head.

Shona's breath stopped.

"Dad!" She rushed to him and fell to her knees at his side. "Dad?"

Blood streaked down his face, running from his nose, pooling in his thick, silvery hair. His eyes came open as if with great effort, and he tried to speak. Blood speckled his teeth.

Shona forced herself not to cry out. "Dad, hold on. I'll call for help." She reached for the cordless desk phone. It wasn't in its cradle. Dad must have tried to call for help and dropped it somewhere. She pulled her cell phone from her purse and punched in 911.

"Shot..." her father murmured, his voice a hushed croak.

"What do you mean? Did someone shoot you?"

He grimaced, more blood dribbling down his chin. "Get away from...Geoff...."

The dispatcher came on the line, and Shona asked for an ambulance. "My father is badly injured. He says he's been shot." As the dispatcher asked for more information, Dad grabbed her by the arm. His sleeve slid back, and she saw a hideous bruise on his forearm, black and swollen. Shot? He looked as if he'd been beaten.

"Hang on, Dad. Help's coming."

"You need your little one...get...away..." His eyes glazed over and his face fell slack.

"No. Dad, stay with me!"

More blood trickled down his face from his nose. His head fell sideways, and she saw a huge bruise on the side of his face. His whole body was hemorrhaging.

She felt for a pulse at his carotid artery. His heart

was still beating, and his warm breath touched her face when she leaned close.

"Please," she said to the dispatcher over the telephone. "My father is in bad shape. Tell them to hurry."

As the voice reassured her that help would be there soon, Shona wanted to scream. Soon might be too late.

TWO

Geoff Tremaine faced the camera and read the final words of the evening newscast from the teleprompter. His image would continue to be present for a few moments in homes throughout the central Missouri viewing area. It was a concept to which he still had not grown completely accustomed, and he tended to avoid watching himself on television.

He said good-night and held his smile until the lights dimmed.

Once, the camera crew had continued filming after the director told them to cut, and Geoff's coanchor had made a snide comment about the governor. That coanchor no longer had a job with this station. Competition was fierce in the broadcasting business; deadly mistakes were not tolerated.

Because of the competition, Geoff considered himself fortunate to be an anchor after working full-time at Channel 6 for only a year. He tried to convince himself that his split with Kemper Mac-

Donald had not been the reason he'd landed the job, but sometimes he wondered. Most television stations preferred younger talent. Though thirty-eight wasn't exactly over the hill, television cameras did tend to emphasize age.

He knew he had established himself here; he now carried his own weight. Nonetheless, he had always suspected that his initial employment with this station had come about because the director, Wendy Phillips, had long held animosity toward Kemper MacDonald.

His coworkers had implied she might have had other reasons, as well. Tall and statuesque, with a strong will and the ability to lead a diverse news team, Wendy usually got what she wanted. She had never made a secret of the fact that she found him attractive.

Geoff loosened his tie and shrugged out of his sport coat before opening the door to his dressing room. The lights on the set were hot, and one of the challenges during the show was to keep perspiration to a minimum.

Before he could step through the door, a familiar contralto called to him from the hallway.

"Heads up, Tremaine. We need you on a scene."

He turned to see Wendy quick-stepping toward him, her face slightly flushed with that familiar, excited look she got when a good story landed in her lap. Wendy was considered beautiful by most standards, with her slightly tilted dark eyes and fiery highlights in her golden brown hair. Geoff had always kept her at arm's length, even more so in the past few weeks.

"Sally just called from the scanner room," she said, as always stepping slightly too close, invading his personal space. "There's an ambulance on its way to Kemper MacDonald's address."

Geoff stiffened. "Kemper? What happened?"

"They say his daughter called 911." Wendy's perfume, with a hint of sweet spice, wafted around her even at the end of a long day. "The senator's been injured. His daughter reported something about a shooting, so I'm sure the police are already swarming the place."

Geoff reached back to the rack for his coat and pulled it on again. "Someone shot Kemper? What about Shona? Is she okay?"

"Nothing was said about her, it's the senator everyone will be concerned about."

He tossed her a glance over his shoulder. "You do realize we're talking about my wife." He heard the chill in his voice, but was unable to warm it, even as Wendy's eyes narrowed at him. She always demanded respect for her authority, brooking no argument from anyone—except, occasionally, from him. He didn't exploit his advantage, but he did disagree with her when he felt it was appropriate.

"I thought you were divorced," she said.

"Separated." Big difference. At least, to him. "I care very much about what happens to my wife."

Wendy's dark gaze slid away from him. "Obviously if she's the one who called for help, she's okay. They're taking Senator MacDonald to Bradley-Cline Hospital. Why don't you go intercept them?"

"Why Bradley-Cline? St. Mary's is closer."

"That isn't our concern. We have a camera crew out right now, so I'll send them to meet you there. You know other stations will already be scrambling to get their crews to the hospital, to try to get a statement from the doctor or the daughter or any other family members who might be there."

"What about the mansion?"

"We'll be covering that, too. I want you at the hospital."

"I'm on my way, but I warn you, this is still my family, and I may not be the most unbiased—"

"Just get there." Her impatience surfaced with her words. "You'll have an insider's view that no other station can provide, and the whole region knows about your relationship with Shona. We've got the advantage."

Geoff winced at the eagerness in her voice as he turned to leave.

"Let me know as soon as you find out anything," Wendy called as he rushed down the hallway. "And take a recorder with you. The hospital won't allow a camera crew into the ER."

He grimaced. She was hallucinating if she thought he would stick a tape recorder under his father-in-law's nose at the hospital and ask him how he felt.

They called that kind of interviewing technique "a Sally" at the station because once, in the field, Channel 6's reporter, Sally Newton, had held a microphone in the face of a man who was watching his home burn with his wife in it. In the excitement of the moment, Sally had not only betrayed her eagerness for a story, but had neglected to school her face to show proper respect for the man's agony. She'd smiled pertly for the camera, and the man's mother had promptly socked her in her pretty mouth.

Sally Newton's public exposure had been greatly reduced since then.

As soon as Geoff climbed into his truck, he set his cell phone on its cradle and hit Shona's speed dial.

Shona's hands shook so badly she could barely hold on to the steering wheel. She was guided only by the flashing lights on the big, boxy ambulance in front of her as it led the way to Bradley-Cline Hospital.

Would Dad even make it there? The blood had been so horrifying…so much of it.

What would cause a person to bleed out like that?

Her cell phone beeped. It was the VIP chime for a high-priority number. Only two people had numbers programmed to that particular tune. One was a passenger in the ambulance ahead of her. This caller could only be Geoff.

With shaking hands, Shona pulled the phone from her pocket, ignoring the hands-free law, and brought the phone to her face. "Geoff?"

"Are you okay?"

The deep timbre of his voice, filled with concern, forged past her controls. Tears sprang to her eyes. The road blurred before her. "I can't talk right now. Dad's…something's wrong with him."

"A report said he'd been shot. How bad is it?"

"There was no sign of an entry wound." The paramedics hadn't wasted a lot of time looking, but if there were a wound, it would have been bleeding. Every orifice in his body seemed to be hemorrhaging, but no bullet wound was evident. "The police are inspecting the mansion."

"Is there someone with you?"

"No, I was told a detective will join me at the hospital."

"I'm on my way there now."

She frowned. Of course, Geoff would have already been informed about it. Breaking news was his business, and there were scanners at the station to get a jump on anything newsworthy. She hadn't thought about that. The hospital would be crawling with reporters looking for her.

She wasn't well acquainted with Bradley-Cline. It was the newest, state-of-the-art hospital in the area that had begun to give St. Mary's and Capitol Region

Medical Center some relief for their overworked staffs and overburdened facilities.

"Geoff, don't make this a public spectacle."

"You know I'll do my best to keep any interviews tasteful and gentle."

She caught her tongue between her teeth. She wasn't up to this. "Look, I'm barely functioning. You either come to the hospital as a concerned family member, or stay away."

"Someone will show up anyway. Wouldn't you rather it be me?"

"Why would I?"

"Because I'll keep everything off the record that you want off the record, and I won't misquote you. I wouldn't be doing this, but Wendy's pulling rank."

"If you come to the hospital as a reporter, you'll be treated as a reporter. You're not taking advantage of your connection to me in order to build ratings for Wendy Phillips."

"That isn't the reason I'm coming."

"Then leave your job at the door, just as you asked me to do, Geoffrey Tremaine."

"Shona, I want to be there for you. At the same time, I don't want someone else approaching you from my station. Reports will be made, one way or the other. I want to give a fair one, for your sake, and for Kemper's."

She knew his argument made sense. "Off the record, I don't know if Dad's even going to make it to the hospital," she said. Brake lights flashed ahead. She barely saw them in time to stop. Her tires squealed. Why weren't they taking her father to the closest hospital? St. Mary's was excellent.

"I'll call Karah Lee for you," Geoff said.

"No," she snapped. "Stay out of this."

"You shouldn't be alone, and your sister deserves to know what's happening."

"Why?" Karah Lee had chosen to distance herself from their father from the moment of Mom and Dad's divorce. Not only had she refused financial assistance from Dad for college, but she had also, in a fit of rebellion that had broken Dad's heart, taken her mother's maiden name. She barely knew Dad's second wife, Irene. To be fair, neither did Shona. The woman had taken little interest in her stepdaughters. And now, Dad and Irene were separated. Shona had no intention of calling her, either.

"This isn't your affair anymore, Geoff," Shona said.

"I'm still family. I'll see you at the hospital in a few minutes," he said gently. "Meanwhile, I'll call Karah Lee."

"Geoff, I don't—"

He disconnected. She started to toss her cell phone on the seat beside her. Instead, she dialed 911 again.

"Yes, this is Shona Tremaine. I'm currently following the ambulance unit 948 to Bradley-Cline Hospital. I need you to contact that ambulance via private line and redirect them to St. Mary's. That's where I want my father taken. It's closer. Also would you redirect the police to St. Mary's, on a private line, as well? I don't want anyone else to know my father's location." Not Geoff. Not Karah Lee. Not Irene.

After the dispatcher agreed to do as she asked—sometimes political power had its perks—Shona expressed her thanks, disconnected and tossed the phone onto the seat, focusing on the lights ahead.

Geoff Tremaine could cool his heels at the fancy new hospital. Meanwhile, Dad would have the best of care at a place she trusted. She should have insisted on St. Mary's from the beginning.

THREE

Karah Lee Fletcher sat in front of the picture window in her lakeside cottage on the edge of Hideaway. She tried hard not to be distracted by the magnificent purples and deep indigoes of the evening sky at late sunset. There was work to be done.

This evening, it was her job to look fascinated by the display of material samples spread out before her on the coffee table. Bored already, she tapped her foot in time with the music her foster daughter had playing on the CD.

"I'm not wearing pink." Fawn held up a swatch of hot pink satin. "Unless it's this."

Karah Lee tore her gaze from the window scene and studied the brilliant, shimmery material. "Looks good to me."

Fawn rolled her eyes. "Do you realize how badly this color would clash with that red hair of yours?"

"So? You'd be the one wearing it, not me."

"But you'll be the bride. Everything should focus

on you on your wedding day. You're one of those people who should never be allowed out on the street before they check in with the fashion police."

"And you, of course, would be my own personal fashion police, I suppose."

"Well, sure, you can do that now, but what are you going to do when I'm in college this fall?" Fawn combed her fingers through her short blond hair, eyeing Karah Lee with a devious grin.

"I guess I'll just have to live in my scrubs. You'll be home in the evenings, so you can prevent disaster."

"Only if you can get me a car before I start school. I can't exactly walk there from here."

"You can use my car or ride with Blaze." Since Karah Lee merely had to walk across the street and up two blocks for work and groceries, she seldom needed to drive these days.

Fawn grumbled, but she did so with good nature. By the time she started college, Karah Lee and Taylor would be married. Fawn had made it clear that the wedding was going to be her priority from now until the final vows were spoken. Thanks to Fawn, heaven and everyone in Hideaway knew Karah Lee wasn't capable of planning and executing a wedding of the caliber everyone expected without a great deal of help from friends.

Karah Lee was not a style maven, nor did she wish to become one at this stage of her life. At thirty-four, she was set in her ways and happy with that.

Fawn's entry into her life still filled her with awe and gratitude. As a sixteen-year-old runaway last year, Fawn had witnessed a murder in Branson—one of the last places on earth one would expect a murder. When she had arrived here in Hideaway—a stowaway on a tour bus filled with senior citizens—she'd been sick, in the middle of a miscarriage.

Karah Lee had become her guardian with a great deal of trepidation, after discovering that the teenager's home life was unbearable. Her mother didn't want her back.

What a blessing Fawn Morrison had been in Karah Lee's life since then.

The telephone rang before Fawn could launch into a long-winded explanation about why she needed her own car, and her plan about how to pay for it while working at the school for her tuition.

Karah Lee answered quickly. "This is Dr. Fletcher."

"Karah Lee?" came a familiar male voice. It was her brother-in-law.

"Geoff?"

"I take it Shona hasn't called you."

At the sound of urgency in Geoff's voice, and the mention of her sister's name, Karah Lee braced herself. Typically, when a phone call concerned her family, things got tense in a hurry.

"What's wrong?" she asked.

"Your father is being taken to the hospital at this moment."

"What happened? Where's Shona?"

"She's on her way there, as well. I'm not sure what's wrong with him yet. Earlier, it was suggested he might have been shot."

Karah Lee's grip tightened on the receiver. "Shot? Like, with a gun?"

Fawn looked up, then got up from the table and walked to Karah Lee's side. "What is it?" she whispered.

Karah Lee placed a hand on her arm, more for strength than to silence her.

"I'm sorry," Geoff said. "I don't know more than that. As I said, Shona is on her way to the hospital. She isn't doing well. You know she doesn't get rattled easily." There was a pause. "She isn't sure Kemper's going to make it."

Karah Lee caught her breath. Shona thought Dad's life was in danger?

"Karah Lee, is there any way you could—"

"I'll be on my way shortly."

"It's a little after seven now." There was a pause. "You might want to be prepared for the worst."

At that moment, Karah Lee realized that she never would be.

Shona rushed to the ER reception desk, breathless from her run from the parking lot. "I need to see my father, Kemper MacDonald. He was just brought in by ambulance."

"Oh, ma'am, I'm sorry," the secretary said gently. "Your father is in critical condition in the trauma room. They're doing everything they—"

Shona saw the door to the ER swing open as someone stepped out. She rushed forward and grabbed it before it could close and lock her out.

An older nurse looked up from her work at the busy central desk and intercepted Shona. "May I help you?"

"I need to find the trauma—" Shona spotted a room where several medical personnel were gathered and headed in that direction.

"I'm sorry," the nurse said, rushing forward to catch her by the arm. "You can't go in there right now. We'll call a chaplain and show you to the family waiting room."

"Kemper MacDonald is my father. My name is Shona Tremaine."

"I know who you are, ma'am. I've seen you on the news."

Shona tried to pull free, but found the woman surprisingly strong. "Please, I need to get to him."

"Not right now, you don't," the nurse assured her gently. "They're attempting to resuscitate him."

Shona gasped. The room threatened to fade around her. "Resuscitate! He's *dead?*"

"I assure you, they're doing everything they can. He's unresponsive right now. We'll do our best to keep you updated."

"Please." Shona took a deep breath to steady

herself. "I need to be there. The doctor may have questions only I can answer. I live with my father, and I know more about him than anyone. I promise not to get in the way."

The woman's grip eased slightly, the lines around her brown eyes deepening as she focused on Shona, as if to measure her words. "It isn't a pretty sight."

"I'm the one who found him. I don't expect it to be pleasant."

The nurse nodded and released Shona's arm, though with obvious reluctance. "You can stand by the window over there, but don't get in the doorway. There'll be people coming in and out."

"The press may come looking for me here. Would you please not give out any information about my father?"

"It's against federal regulations to do so, Mrs. Tremaine. Anyone who does will be fired."

Shona nodded. "Thank you. My…husband may show up looking for me. His name is—"

"Geoff Tremaine? He won't be hard to recognize. Do you want us to let him know where you are?"

She wanted her *husband,* Geoff, not the reporter. She sighed. "If he does show up, it's okay, but no camera team, and no one except Geoff."

"We wouldn't do it any other way."

Shona thanked her. She knew her switch wouldn't deter him for long. He would figure out soon enough where she had taken Dad.

Steeling herself for what she might see, Shona rushed to the trauma room and tried to peer in the glass windows through small gaps between the slats in a blind.

She could see little except medical equipment, a monitor and people in multicolored scrubs and masks standing around the trauma bed. She strained to hear anything encouraging through the verbal cacophony that filtered through the door.

"Central line is in. Stop CPR. What's the rhythm?"

"Still PEA."

Shona caught her breath. She'd learned enough from her sister to know that meant pulseless electrical activity.

Very bad.

"Continue CPR."

"Got it."

"We need to push some volume back into his circulation. Get that O negative blood in now. How much longer on those four units of fresh frozen plasma?"

"Lab said just a few more minutes. They have to thaw them first."

"Where's the 20 milligrams of vitamin K? I wanted it stat."

"Right here, Dr. Morris."

"Give it IV push."

"But doctor, what about the risk—"

"I'm not worried about the risk of anaphylactic shock at this point, Carrie." There was tension in the doctor's voice. "He's bleeding to death, and we don't know what's causing it. He needs it IV. *Now.* And someone see if there's a family member here who knows what's going on."

Shona caught her breath. "I'm his daughter!" she called, stepping to the door. She gasped, suddenly overwhelmed by what she saw.

Blood. There was blood everywhere, on the bed, on Dad's body, on the hands of the staff, on the instruments they were using on Dad's hideously battered flesh.

Without warning, a wave of nausea overwhelmed her. She turned away, doubling over, fighting to keep her gorge down.

Someone caught her from behind and placed a basin in front of her just in time.

"That's why we don't like people coming back at times like this," came the gentle-sad voice of the older nurse as Shona gave up all pretense of dignity.

Past humiliation, Shona retched, miserable and terrified. No one could bleed as much as Dad was doing and live. She was losing him.

Geoff raced into the parking lot of the ER at Bradley-Cline Hospital and pulled into a nearby slot, scanning the area for Shona's Escalade or Kemper's Seville, which she often drove. He recognized none of the vehicles.

He frowned at the ambulance bay. There was no

way he could have beat the ambulance here, but he couldn't have been so far behind them that the ambulance was already gone, could he?

It was possible, if they had another hot call.

Still...something didn't feel right. Shona's car should be here. She had been following the ambulance when he spoke to her; he'd heard the siren over the line.

She might have parked elsewhere in an effort to avoid notice, as much as possible. Her car and Kemper's had government plates.

While waiting for the camera crew, Geoff parked and went inside to check with the receptionist.

"I'm sorry," she said when he asked about Kemper's arrival. "We're unaware of anyone here by that name."

He didn't argue, but returned to his car, backed out of the slot and cruised slowly around the parking lot. He saw nothing familiar. He dialed Shona's number again, but she didn't answer. He did recognize a film crew from Channel 32, and a newspaper reporter for the *Jefferson City Herald*. He was sure more reporters would be arriving soon.

His own camera crew had not yet made it here, and he had a sneaking suspicion they wouldn't have anything to film once they arrived. He knew Shona too well. She didn't want a media circus tonight.

Typically, she was gracious and outgoing to all members of the media, as was her father. This was different. He couldn't blame her for wanting her privacy during this crisis.

Instead of calling Wendy, which he knew would be expected of him with this switch, he pulled from the parking lot and turned left, in the direction of St. Mary's. Traditionally, Shona's family had always used that hospital. He would follow his hunch without alerting others.

FOUR

After the nurse carried away the basin, Shona collapsed gratefully in a chair someone pushed over from the central desk.

Another member of medical staff in bloodstained blue scrubs knelt beside her, his eyes compassionate, but his tone brisk. "Ma'am, does your father have any history of hemophilia?"

"No." Didn't he think she would have told them immediately if that were the case?

"Does he take any kind of blood thinner like Coumadin? Or a lot of aspirin?"

"Nothing like that. He seldom even takes a painkiller." Shona accepted some wet paper towels from an aide and dabbed at her face and mouth.

"Has he been ill recently, running a high fever?"

"No. He had a cold, but nothing serious. Please, do you know what's happening?"

The man shook his head. "That's what we're still trying to find out." He returned to the trauma room.

"Got something here, Dr. Morris," someone said. "He could be coming back around. We've got a better rhythm."

"Stop CPR. Is there a pulse?"

There was a waiting silence for a few seconds.

"No, Doctor."

"Okay, continue CPR."

Shona couldn't take it. She had always thought she would be strong in a situation like this. She wasn't. She had never felt so alone in her life.

Geoff pulled into St. Mary's parking lot behind a police car. He saw another unmarked car at the curb, and an ambulance hovered in the bay, as if it had recently made a delivery. He was pretty sure he had found the right place, though Shona's vehicle was not in sight.

As he pulled into an empty spot, his cell phone beeped. He checked the screen and saw Wendy's number.

He pressed the talk button. "Wendy, I'm sorry, I can't talk right now. Do you mind if I call you back—"

"Where are you?" Her words were clipped, impatient.

"I'm at the hospital."

"No, you aren't. The crew can't find you."

"I think the ambulance was diverted to another hospital."

"Which one?"

"I'm at St. Mary's right now, but I haven't made it inside, and they have a sign at the entrance that requests we turn all cell phones off. I'll call you as soon as—"

"We didn't hear about it on the scanner."

"They could have used a private line. I'm not sure yet. I'm checking it out now, but it's obvious Shona doesn't want media attention right now."

"She doesn't have the liberty to pick and choose when she receives coverage and when she doesn't," Wendy snapped.

Geoff gritted his teeth. *Careful, Wendy, your antagonism is showing.* "You know the hospital won't allow a crew into the emergency department," he said. "I'm sure Shona won't leave her father's side. On the other hand, there will be lights flashing and police cars lining the street around the MacDonald mansion. What's going to give us better ratings?"

There was a buzzing silence, then a sharp sigh. "Fine. We already have a crew at the mansion, but I need you there to report. I don't want to trust Sally with this."

"Can't Megan or Emily do it? I need to be with my family right now, Wendy."

"You have a job to do, Tremaine. I suggest you follow orders if you want to keep your cushy position with all its perks."

He swallowed a sharp retort. "Think about the ratings. If Megan comes on the screen live from the

MacDonald mansion, filling in for Geoff Tremaine, who's with his wife and father-in-law at the hospital, don't you think that's going to catch the attention of viewers?"

"Not as well as Geoff Tremaine himself."

"But what if your man on the scene is able to get exclusive, timely updates from the source?"

There was another thoughtful pause. Wendy could ride roughshod over everyone when she wanted her way, but she did, on occasion, accept input. "You're trying to manipulate me."

He got out of the car, locked it, and started toward the ER entrance, dropping his keys into his right front pocket. "Is it working?"

Another sigh. "Call me when you find something out. Anything."

"Thanks, Wendy, you're all heart."

"No, I just want that exclusive. Make time while you can. The others will catch on soon enough."

He disconnected and slid the phone into his jacket pocket.

Shona looked up to see a man coming toward her. He wore a navy suit without a tie, and she recognized him as a police detective with whom she had spoken a couple of times in the past.

"Mrs. Tremaine? I don't know if you remember me, but I'm Detective Milt Davis. Are you okay?" He bent toward her, his eyes filled with concern.

She nodded and stood, reaching to shake his hand, allowing her public persona to settle into place even as the hospital crew battled for her father's life. It felt like a physical weight.

"Of course, Milt. You've called me Shona in the past. I hope that hasn't changed."

The man was tall and slender, with graying hair around the temples and a lined face that emphasized his fiftysomething years of age combined with long hours on the force. He glanced toward the trauma room, where the staff continued to work over their patient. At least, they were still working.

"Thank you for calling to alert us to your change of location. I hate to interrupt you at a time like this," he said, "but when you called for help initially, you suggested that this might have been a shooting. If that's so, we need to follow any leads we can find as quickly as possible."

"I'll tell you everything I can," she said. "Which is very little."

Milt Davis spoke briefly with a nearby nurse, then led Shona to a conference room down the corridor.

"I'm afraid I'm not focusing very well," Shona said, seating herself in a vinyl chair at the table.

"That's understandable." He took out his recorder and a notebook and asked her permission to tape their conversation. "Tell me what happened."

"Dad wasn't very coherent when I found him, and what he said didn't make sense to me. If he was shot, no one has found a bullet wound. The blood was everywhere, coming from his nose, his teeth, bruising under his skin, but no wound, so that makes it clear to me that he must have been talking about something else."

"Don't worry, I'll walk you through this. I know it's been awful for you, but just because there is no evidence of a shooting doesn't mean we're willing to rule out foul play. When did you first notice something was wrong?"

Karah Lee pressed her foot on the imaginary brake on the passenger's side, gripping the armrest with her right hand. "Fawn, it's a good four hours to Jefferson City on a clear day. Don't try to make it in an hour at night."

"I can do it in less than four. You drive like my great-grandma."

"She's probably still alive, too. Which we won't be if you don't slow down."

Instead of arguing as she normally did, Fawn allowed the car to slow enough that they took the next curve on all four wheels. Karah Lee loosened her death grip on the armrest and flexed the cramping muscles of her right foot.

"You doing okay?" Fawn asked.

"I'm trying not to think about things. It would help if I could drive."

"You're upset. You don't need to be distracted

with driving when you're so upset. Older people don't focus as well as—"

"Don't start with me, young lady. Thirty-four isn't old. You're just looking for an excuse to drive, and I think using my anxiety as an excuse is reprehensible."

"How can you say that when—"

"Slow down. Don't forget four-legged creatures reign over this road at night." Karah Lee felt herself relax in spite of Fawn's aggressive driving. She suspected that had been Fawn's purpose from the beginning—that and her natural urge, like every teenager's, to sit behind the controls of a speeding vehicle.

"We should have packed more." Fawn made a cursory show of braking and turned onto Highway 76. "What if your father's in the hospital for a while? All we have is an overnight case."

Karah Lee swallowed hard, staring ahead at the glow of headlights from a car coming over the next hill. "You should concentrate on driving right now."

From the corner of her eye she saw Fawn look at her.

"Keep your eyes on the road."

"I'm watching the road. Haven't you been praying all these months that Kemper would see the error of his ways and change them?"

Karah Lee winced. That sounded so…fundamentally Christian. Of course, she *was* fundamentally Christian, but…

"I've been told often enough that if I pray for something in God's will, He gives it to me. Don't you think it's God's will for Kemper to get to know Him?" Fawn dimmed her headlights for the oncoming car, then when the oncoming lights didn't dim, she muttered, "Jerk! You're trying to blind me!"

Karah Lee reached for the seat belt and tightened it, once more pressing her imaginary brake. Why didn't cars come equipped with optional brakes on the passenger's side, too? They did that on driver's-ed vehicles.

The car passed without mishap.

"So, where's your faith?" Fawn asked.

Karah Lee sighed and sat back. It was hard to imagine that her father might have had a change of heart after all these years. She had noticed, however, that his attitude seemed to have undergone a change when he met his son for the first time.

Jerrod Houston, her newly discovered illegitimate brother, had been a shock to the great State Senator Kemper MacDonald. Karah Lee hoped it wasn't her imagination that her father had encountered an authority more powerful than himself as he sought to make peace with his past.

She only wished she knew what to expect next.

FIVE

Geoff sat in the crowded waiting room, watching the inner door for Shona to come out and the outer door for the first news crews to arrive.

Shona was unreachable right now, in conference with the police. Ordinarily, the hospital personnel wouldn't have told him even that much, except Shona had left word for him. At least she had relented somewhat.

He still wasn't sure what his reception would be when he and Shona met. They had parted on a note of anger last year, and nothing that had passed between them in eleven months had given Geoff any reason to think she had had a change of heart. He, on the other hand, had endured plenty of second thoughts. Why had he been so demanding?

And yet, he still meant what he'd said. For several years, Shona had been evolving into her father's puppet, scrambling to do whatever it took to keep Kemper MacDonald content. She had overlooked more and more of Kemper's unethical behavior, even when he lied, manipulated and ingratiated himself to win votes to assure the completion of his own agenda. Until a couple of weeks ago, that agenda had been the advancement of his own career—and Shona's.

It was at that time, during a private, late-night visit from his father-in-law, that Geoff had discovered a thread of hope that all was not lost.

Geoff checked again with the receptionist at the ER desk and was told that Kemper was still in critical condition. At least he was alive.

An older lady stood behind Geoff when he turned around. "Mr. Tremaine?"

"Yes, ma'am."

She held her checkbook out with one hand, an ink pen with the other. "Could I get your autograph? This is all I could find to write on."

He hesitated. He had never been able to fathom why anyone would be interested in his autograph, but Wendy insisted it was good PR. With a smile, he relented and did as he was asked. He signed with a flourish he had practiced, the writing as much unlike his normal writing style as he could make it in order to protect himself from identity theft—good advice from an attorney who had visited the station.

"Do you have someone in the ER tonight?" he asked the lady as he handed her the signed book.

She nodded. "My mother. She has congestive heart failure. I just saw you over here and—"

"I'm sorry to hear about that."

"Oh, she'll recover as soon as they pull off the fluid. They've done it before."

"I hope she'll be okay."

The lady gazed up at him. "Thank you, Mr. Tremaine," she said on a sigh. "You know, I never miss the Channel 6 news now that you're there."

He smiled, refusing to take the woman's admiration seriously.

As the lady returned to her seat, Geoff realized he and Shona had always been two of a kind. They lived in the public eye, and though they didn't particularly enjoy the attention their jobs brought them, they had learned to cope with the fish-bowl syndrome years ago.

At least, most of the time.

To his relief, Shona stepped through the door from the ER. She spotted him immediately and started toward him, looking very tense. He knew that look well.

Though his wife had always been beautiful, the years had graced her, giving her a polish that didn't fully emerge until her midthirties. She now had silver-blond highlights in her short, thick dark hair, and her eyes, which had always been large, no longer made her appear ingenuous but astute. Amazing what a few years of seasoning could do for a woman. She was more beautiful than ever.

Unfortunately for him, she was also less easy to read.

He was stepping forward to meet her when the entry door opened, admitting Sally Newton and a cameraman from the station.

Sally, spotting Shona, wove her way through the crowded room. "Mrs. Tremaine, can you tell us how the senator is doing?"

All eyes in the waiting room suddenly focused on Shona.

Sally was in her midtwenties, and she had not yet learned many lessons in diplomacy. She advanced on Shona with a microphone in her hand, gesturing for the cameraman to follow her.

Shona raised a hand of entreaty toward Geoff. "Please, not now," she said softly. "I can't talk right—"

"Sal," Geoff said, smoothly stepping in front of Shona to shield her from the camera, "the senator's family will have a statement for the press as soon as possible. At this moment we don't have sufficient information to relay, only that Senator MacDonald is in critical condition."

The pretty blonde blinked at him. "But Wendy told me—"

Shona took Geoff's arm.

"We'll contact you as soon as we have a statement," he told the reporter. "You must understand our concerns. Shona needs to focus all her attention on her father at this time."

"Can you at least tell us what happened? Was this a murder attempt?" Sally asked.

Geoff heard Shona catch her breath at the question. He lowered his voice. "I just told you, Sally, that there will be a statement later. There's nothing here for you to see." Without staying to argue, he ushered Shona back through the doors into the bustling ER.

"That young woman needs to learn some manners," Shona snapped.

"As Wendy would say, she's simply doing her job."

"I'm sure that's exactly what Wendy would say. I'm just glad you decided there was something more important at the…moment…." Shona stopped, gazing toward the trauma room where a team of hospital personnel surrounded someone—Kemper? Her hand tightened on Geoff's arm.

"We don't need to be here right now," he said. "Is there a private room where we can wait?"

She led him along a corridor to a conference room with a table and chairs, love seat and recliner.

She released his arm at last, and sank onto the love seat. He resisted the urge to assure her that everything would be okay. He'd learned long ago not to make assurances he couldn't keep, especially to Shona Tremaine, who would not hesitate to call him on it.

"How are you doing?" he asked.

She grimaced. "I discovered I don't handle medical emergencies well. Karah Lee would be ashamed of me. I held together until I tried to watch them work on Dad in the trauma room." She wiggled her fingers in front of her stomach, giving him a good idea about what had happened.

"I called her," Geoff said. "She's on her way."

Those large, dark gray eyes narrowed. "I asked you not to do that."

"She's his daughter, too, and she's coming. Give her some credit."

Shona's grimace told him she was irritated but not really angry. He hadn't pushed it too far…yet.

"Only because you called," she said. "Karah Lee likes you better than she does me."

"You know that isn't true."

"Of course, it is." She glanced up at him, then quickly looked away. "She even told me that once."

"You two are always pulling each other's chains." Shona retained her privacy with dignity in the public eye, but, despite their separation, she seemed to be as candid as always with him. The key word was *seemed.* He no longer knew if he could take her at her word, especially since he knew she felt she must be on guard with him.

"How did it go with the police?" he asked.

"Is this Geoffrey Tremaine, reporter for Channel 6 news asking, or Geoff, my husband?"

"It's always just me, Shona."

She leaned forward. "And who, exactly, is that? When I spoke with you on the phone you seemed determined to interview me."

"And you were just as determined not to be interviewed. You gave me no choice. For me, family has to come first."

She blinked and looked away, and he realized, belatedly, the effect his words would have on her.

"That's laudable." Her voice had suddenly gone soft.

"I'm sorry, Shona. I wasn't trying to—"

"For me, it seems I allowed the job, and my father, to come first."

"I didn't mean—"

"Milt Davis interviewed me," she said. "Then he warned me the mansion will remain a crime scene until further notice. The FBI might be stepping in if the evidence suggests the attack on Dad—if that's what happened—could be political in nature."

"Did Milt give you any indication whether or not the police thought that could be the case?"

"We don't know what happened yet. Dad is just bleeding for no reason, bruising beneath his skin, as if his clotting factor has suddenly failed."

"That isn't a naturally occurring event," Geoff said. "I know your father doesn't have hemophilia."

"That's why the police are suspicious of foul play. I'm sure they're looking for a weapon at the house, but I don't know of anything that would cause that kind of bleeding."

"You won't be able to stay at the mansion, obviously."

She shook her head. "I don't want to leave here

anyway while Dad's critical. A policewoman is going to pack some things and bring them by for me later. I'll stay at The Capitol Plaza."

"You can come home with me. You'll be safer there."

She looked up at him, her eyes misting. Then she dropped her gaze and shook her head. "Not this way," she said softly.

He sat down in the chair across from her. "Did anyone actually see a wound?"

"No. As much as Dad was bleeding, the doctor would have seen blood coming from a specific wound, but there was nothing."

"Where did you get the idea that this was a shooting?"

"He said the word," Shona told him. "He said, 'Shot.'"

"That's it?"

She spread her hands. "Then he said for me to…" She gave him a quick glance, then looked down at her fingers. "He said to get away."

"From what? From him? Why would he—"

"He might have been trying to tell me to get out of Jefferson City."

"What else did he say?" Geoff asked.

She didn't look at him. "I think he must have been hallucinating. He said something about getting the little one out…I'm not sure exactly what he said. It made no sense."

Geoff studied her expression as she continued to avoid eye contact. What was she *not* telling him?

His cell phone rang, and he groaned. He was supposed to turn it off when he entered the hospital. In the excitement, he had ignored the sign, even after mentioning it to Wendy.

To his relief, he saw the caller was not Wendy, nor did the number belong to anyone else with his news team. It was Linda Plinkett, Kemper's old friend, fellow committee member on the Drug Task Force, and, quite possibly, a whole lot more. He answered in spite of the hospital policy restricting cell phones, knowing there were no machines in this section of the building that would be disrupted by the electronic transmission.

"Yes, Linda?"

"Geoffrey Tremaine, what on earth is happening to Kemper? I just heard on the news that he's been shot!"

"He's still in critical condition."

"Where? I can't reach Shona."

"We're here at the hospital."

"Which hospital? I can't find him, and these blasted federal regulations prevent the hospital staff from telling me where he is."

Geoff glanced at Shona. "We're at St. Mary's." Linda might as well jump into the investigation with both feet. She would be embroiled in it soon enough.

"I'll be right there," she said.

* * *

Shona couldn't face Geoff with the swift rush of suspicion that held her mute. Dad couldn't have been talking about Geoff. He must have meant Jefferson City. Longtime residents often called it just plain "Jeff."

She hugged herself, unable to stop shivering. How many times would she have to repeat Dad's words in the next few days? Geoff was bound to hear it from someone. The police would want to question him, if only because of that one statement Dad made.

And yet, she couldn't bring herself to tell Geoff. For these few moments, they were being more civil with each other than they had been since before their separation. She didn't want to break the spell because of her inability to trust.

Geoff stood up and shrugged out of his sport coat, then gently placed it around her shoulders. She could smell the warm, woodsy scent of his aftershave as his hands rested briefly on her shoulders.

It would be so comforting to allow him to take care of everything.

That was impossible, of course. Too many issues remained between them to simply erase the past. And besides, there was this suspicion….

Instead of returning to his chair, Geoff sat on the arm of the love seat. "Do you have any idea what your father might have been talking about? What did he want you to get away from?"

"He was practically incoherent, and he lost consciousness while he was still talking. He could have even been hallucinating."

"But you got the impression he was warning you about something?"

She glanced up at him. Why did he insist on pursuing the subject? "I didn't get any impressions at all at the time, okay, Geoff?" she said more sharply than she'd intended. "He was bleeding badly. All I cared about was getting help."

"The police are combing the mansion for evidence of a crime. It would be foolhardy to consider going alone to a hotel room if there is any danger at all. Can't we forget the issues between us long enough to see this through? Your safety is more important than—"

She raised a hand to silence him. "Dad's in the other room, fighting for his life. That's all I can think about." She wrapped his coat around her more tightly and stood up. She never had been able to sit still in a crisis.

She glanced over her shoulder at Geoff. Her husband could be a model for a clean-cut, all-American grown-up Boy Scout. His blue eyes were clear beneath straight, light brown eyebrows. She knew him so well, had known him for so long, since they were love-struck teenagers in high school. So why did he suddenly seem like a stranger to her? Not a stranger, exactly, but…somehow different.

She reached into her pocket for some change, but

it was empty. She had locked her purse in her car. Why had she done that?

"Coffee?" he asked.

She nodded. "Anything to take this sour taste out of my mouth."

He pulled some coins from the pocket of his slacks. "I'll be right back."

She watched him leave, then paced the room, unable to sit down. There were no windows, and suddenly the walls seemed too confining, suffocating.

For the first time in years, Shona considered prayer. She dismissed the idea immediately, but she understood why people turned to God in times of distress.

How good it would feel—how comforting—to be able to allow someone else to take the load from her that she always seemed to be carrying. But was there anyone to take it? She'd shouldered the weight alone for so long with no help from anyone.

Okay, maybe Geoff had tried to share her burdens, but he always insisted on doing things his way. That had been one of the problems between them. They handled situations so differently.

Moments later, he stepped back into the room with two mugs of coffee. "The nurse took pity on us."

"Thanks." Shona took one and inhaled the steam that rose from the hot liquid.

"Cream, no sugar," he said. "I tried to get you decaf, but that pot was empty. You have enough to worry about without more stress. Are you still trying to cut back on caffeine?"

She knew he was trying to distract her. He'd always been good at that. And she had often resented the tactic. "Trying, but I haven't—"

The door opened, and in stepped the doctor who had led her father's medical team. Shona froze.

"Mrs. Tremaine? I'm Dr. Morris." He wore a fresh, white coat, but his green scrubs were still bloodstained.

"Yes, Doctor," Shona said. "How is my father?"

Dr. Morris gestured for Shona and Geoff to sit on the love seat. He sat across from them on the recliner. "I've asked our hospital chaplain to join us. He's on his way."

Shona felt her strength drain away at his words. "You can just tell us, Doctor. I don't need a preacher to translate for me."

"I'm sorry, Mrs. Tremaine, we did all we could to resuscitate your father. He responded for a few minutes, and then succumbed. Kemper MacDonald is dead."

Shona felt herself go numb. She knew medical personnel had to speak that way. Euphemisms for death could lead to misunderstandings. Still, it sounded so harsh.

Geoff placed an arm around her shoulders, and she stiffened, resistant. He'd tried to destroy her relationship with her father. He would not intrude into her grief.

He removed his arm. "Dr. Morris, was there any evidence of a gunshot wound?"

"None."

"When can I see him?" Shona asked.

The doctor shook his head. "I'm sorry, that wouldn't be—"

"I won't fall apart on you this time, Dr. Morris. I need to see my father."

There was a long hesitation. "Give us time to clean him up, Mrs. Tremaine. We don't want to cause you any more grief than necessary."

"Do you have any idea yet what might have killed him?" Geoff asked.

The doctor shook his head. "There will be an autopsy, of course. That should give us some answers." He gently touched Shona's shoulder. "The chaplain will help you with the final arrangements. Again, I'm very sorry for your loss."

She nodded and leaned her head against the sofa. Dad was dead. There was no going back. He was gone.

SIX

Karah Lee received the call as Fawn exited I-44 and headed north toward Lake of the Ozarks. It was Geoff.

"How far out are you?" he asked.

"Couple of hours, maybe less the way Fawn's breaking every speed limit." She cast a glare in Fawn's direction, to no avail. Fawn was resolute. She either wanted to get them to Jefferson City in record time, or she wanted to be mangled in a tragic accident.

"You can slow down now," Geoff said quietly.

Her hand tightened on the tiny phone. "Tell me he's better."

"I'm sorry, Karah Lee, I can't do that."

She didn't want to hear this. Denial would be welcome for a while longer.

"The medical personnel did all they could, but your father couldn't be resuscitated. He's gone."

For a moment, she didn't respond, watching the traffic in front of her. The glare of headlights merged into a string of brilliant pearls as sudden, warm tears tickled her cheeks. *No, Dad. Don't leave this way, not with this thing still between us.*

"Karah Lee?" Geoff said.

"Should we turn around and go back home, then?" She knew that sounded callous, and she didn't mean for it to. She suddenly just felt so…cut off. Adrift. How was Shona feeling?

"No. Come to Jefferson City. You're needed now, more than ever."

"I'm not. It'll be awkward with me there."

"And you don't think it's awkward between Shona and me? Your father is gone, Karah Lee. Your presence is needed here now."

She heard the impatience in his voice. This was hard on him, too. "Sorry, but really, Geoff, my presence there will be stressful for Shona right now, and she doesn't need that."

"You don't have any idea what Shona needs, do you?" Again, the impatience, barely there, and restrained by a strong dose of Geoff Tremaine manners.

"What do you mean?"

"She and I are still legally separated, and there's still tension between us. She just lost her father. There's a murder investigation going on, and—"

Karah Lee gasped. "There really is a murder investigation?"

Fawn gasped, and the car slowed momentarily.

"Yes, and Shona's already been questioned. She

doesn't have anyone close to her here. She needs you, even though she probably doesn't realize it herself."

Again, the headlights seemed to become a stream of attack against Karah Lee's eyes. She didn't know what to say. What would she do when she arrived in Jefferson City?

"You need to be watchful when you arrive, though," he continued. "As I've said, the police suspect your father was murdered."

"Then Fawn shouldn't even be with me."

"Please don't return to Hideaway now, Karah Lee. My home will be secure for you."

"The mansion wasn't safe for Dad, even with all the security measures he took." Karah Lee closed her eyes. Murder was such a horrible word. Who would want to kill Dad? Oh, sure, he was controversial, and politics could be messy, ugly, dirty. Dad had always known how to play the game.

Had he offended someone too many times? Had his political platform threatened someone? In the past few months, Dad had become very outspoken against the illegal methamphetamine situation and had called for more police intervention, stiffer sentences.

Last summer, when Karah Lee called Dad for help against the insidious Beaufont Corporation that was attempting to take over Hideaway, he had ridden into town with the feds like a knight in shining armor and cleaned house. It turned out Beaufont had connections with organized crime. Those people held grudges.

Why hadn't she told him more often that she appreciated his heroics last year? Why had she allowed this gulf to remain between them until it was too late? Yes, they had always clashed. Dad tended to ride roughshod over everyone to get what he wanted, even when it involved meddling in her professional life. She'd resented it. Being her father's daughter, she didn't take his manipulations in silence.

"Karah Lee?" Geoff said, his voice gentle. "Are you okay?"

"I'm not sure." Could her run-in with the Beaufont Corporation last summer have something to do with this? What if she had been the indirect cause of her father's death?

"The police are questioning everyone right now," Geoff said. "Please just come up here. They've taken blood and urine samples for screening. The FBI may take control of this investigation."

She watched the spread of dark Missouri countryside pass around them as Fawn sped into the night. "How's Shona holding up?"

"She seems to have withdrawn from everyone around her, although she's still able to compose herself for the cameras."

"Of course." Shona had always been capable of shoving her feelings aside for the needs of others, and especially for Dad and her work.

"You need to be advised," Geoff said, "that at this

moment, she insists she will stay at the Capitol Plaza, no matter how impractical."

"No surprise there. Any idea how long before anyone can return to the mansion?"

"The investigation is taking time. It could be days."

"Can you convince Shona to stay with you if she knows Fawn and I would be at the house, as well?"

"You don't think I've tried?"

"We can't leave her alone."

"So that means you're coming up?" Geoff asked.

Karah Lee realized he'd worked that to his advantage. "Yes, I guess that's what it means. That is, if Fawn and I aren't in a major traffic accident before we arrive there. Will you call me when you can in the next couple of hours, keep me informed about how things are going?"

"Yes, and I'll let you know if any authorities feel that you and Shona could be in danger."

Karah Lee glanced at Fawn. "Thanks. You be careful, too, Geoff."

After she disconnected she looked at Fawn. "Dad's gone."

"I heard. You okay?"

Karah Lee felt the trembling radiate from deep within her. "I will be."

"They think he was murdered?" Fawn asked.

"They're treating it as a murder investigation, yes. It could be dangerous."

"I thrive on danger."

"Fawn, I should have left you at home."

"You shouldn't be worrying about me, you should be praying for your sister."

"You're my top priority. I want to keep you safe."

"Sure. And I want to make sure to avoid any free-for-all between you and Shona. Are you two going to play nice for once?"

The distraction worked, somewhat. Karah Lee was able to focus on the age-old issue of sibling fending. "Don't expect to find us sharing intimacies during a pajama party."

"We have a funeral to plan," Fawn said.

"I know." Karah Lee didn't want to think about it, couldn't face it yet. "I'm sorry. Let's just talk about it when we get there."

Though Geoff had expected a tense investigation, he hadn't expected a detective to commandeer him so quickly. It had happened mere moments after he had stood beside Shona to make the announcement of Kemper's death to the media crowd outside the main hospital entrance.

Detective Bradley Shane led him back to a private consultation room deep in the maze of the hospital and sat across from him at a round table.

"I'll try not to keep you long, Mr. Tremaine," he said, placing his notebook and a recorder on the table. "I know your wife could use your support right now."

"Thank you." Though the media had pounded

both Shona and himself with questions, they had given no details.

"However," Detective Shane continued, pulling out a chair for himself and indicating that Geoff should do the same, "I understand you and your wife have been separated. How long has that been?"

"Approximately eleven months." It felt much longer. Their lives certainly hadn't developed as they'd expected on their wedding day so many years ago.

"And yet you came to the hospital the moment you heard about the tragedy?"

"Of course." Geoff was getting tired of explaining that his separation from Shona did not cut his ties to her or her family. They had been together too many years for that.

"Would you mind telling me the circumstances of your separation from Mrs. Tremaine?" Shane asked.

"Irreconcilable differences." This guy must not be from around here. The rest of central Missouri seemed intimately acquainted with their situation. Geoff had already heard every conceivable reason for their split.

What the media didn't know was that he didn't want a divorce. He didn't believe in divorce, and he didn't think Shona really wanted one, either. At least, the Shona he had once known would not want one.

"Would you mind elaborating?" Shane asked.

Geoff spread his hands, trying to conceal his impatience. Why was he even here? It wasn't as if he could be a suspect. "Shona and I dated before college, then worked together for Kemper directly out of college before we were married."

"And after you were married? Too much strain?" the man asked, as if he'd heard it all before.

"Not at first. Last year we had a sharp disagreement about the number of hours she spent on the job."

"Workaholic?"

"She tended to put everything into her work."

"If that happened to me, I might hold a grudge against the man for whom she worked," Shane said, watching Geoff closely.

Geoff didn't rise to the bait.

"Mr. Tremaine, can you tell me what your wife's job entailed with her father?"

"She was his executive assistant, and she was what you might call 'in training.' It was obvious to everyone around him for the past few years that he was attempting to groom her for political office herself."

"I hear he once tried to do that with you."

"That's right, but we clashed. I apparently wasn't cut out for politics." At least, not Kemper's brand of politics. "Shona was often his spokesperson with the media and others. She accompanied him everywhere."

"Would you say she was particularly ambitious to take her place in the political field?"

"She was her father's daughter. She's good with people, she's astute and she loves politics." Though he wasn't sure if her attitude might have changed in the past few months, he knew she had, at one point, been intrigued by Kemper's suggestion that she run for his present position when he decided to run for governor.

"How did you feel about that, Mr. Tremaine?" the detective asked.

Geoff frowned. Once upon a time, he had responded with enthusiasm. "I believed she would make a good state senator." Though her future family life would most likely fall by the wayside. But hadn't that already happened?

"So there wasn't any competition between you and Shona?"

"Should there have been? I fully supported Shona's career." Until it destroyed their marriage.

"And your wife? How badly would you say she wanted her father's position?"

"She's always been driven by her work, but if you're asking me if she would kill her father over it, that's impossible. She idolizes her father, no matter what."

"Do you mind telling me why you resigned from his staff?"

"I disagreed with his lifestyle. I felt it would too directly influence his judgment and the impact he would have on the fiscal and ethical health of this state."

The detective frowned at him. "Did you memorize that statement for the media?" he asked dryly.

"No. It's simply the truth."

"Did you and the senator ever have a sharp disagreement?"

"Not since I resigned as his aide. Before that, I made my opinion clear to Kemper on several occasions when I disagreed with his vote in session or with some of the comments he made in public."

"For instance?"

Geoff shrugged. "I didn't appreciate his mudslinging during the last election. I know it happens all the time, but he went overboard and ruined the reputation of his opponent, Randall Phillips, claiming the man had ties to organized crime, though Kemper was never able to provide convincing proof to back up his claims. He used fiction as facts, and people believed it because they believed in him."

"Isn't Phillips the father of your present director at the television station?"

"That's correct. Wendy Phillips is Randall's daughter." The detective had either been doing his homework very quickly or he had been keeping up with the MacDonald saga with the rest of the Missouri heartland. One thing the MacDonalds had was name recognition. Paul Forester had taught Kemper to do that decades ago, and those lessons from his chief advisor had served Kemper well.

"How did you land the position at the television station after your resignation from the senator's staff?" the detective asked.

"That's something you'd have to ask Wendy Phillips."

Shane nodded as he wrote in his notebook.

"During the time you've worked with Ms. Phillips, have you seen any indication that she held a grudge against the senator?"

"She made it obvious she didn't care for him, but I saw to it that she understood before I took the job that I held no ill will toward Kemper, and I would not be used as a tool in any kind of retaliation against him."

"And your wife? Do you know if Shona Tremaine had any disagreements with her father over your separation?"

"Until tonight I haven't been in contact with her since our separation, but I've heard of no disagreements. They always had a good relationship."

"What about the son?" the detective asked.

Geoff was able to keep his reaction to a minimum. "I'm surprised Jerrod Houston's name even arose. He showed up in Hideaway one weekend just before Kemper was scheduled to give a speech there about healthcare. Jerrod presented himself to Kemper as his illegitimate son."

"That must have been quite a shock to the senator."

"Yes, but I don't see how it would relate to Kemper's death. As far as I know, Jerrod held no animosity against his father."

"It isn't my job to make a judgment, Mr. Tremaine, I'm simply gathering as many facts as possible about who might have reason to kill the senator, and we're not being very selective about the possibilities at this point."

"I understand."

"Would you know if Jerrod had a key to the mansion or the knowledge to get past the security system?"

"No, I wouldn't."

"And you would know nothing about his attempt to hack into his sisters' medical files, or his father's?"

"Their medical files? Are you sure about that?" Geoff asked. "I'd heard Jerrod hacked into Karah Lee's personnel file at the clinic to confirm that she was his sister, but why would he hack into their medical files?" And why would the police have information about this?

To Geoff's surprise, the detective closed his notebook. "That'll be all for now. The investigation is open, and I must ask that you stay in town for a few days. I feel sure we'll need to ask you more questions."

"I'll be available."

"You might also take extra safety precautions. A cruiser will spend some extra time on surveillance around your home, but you need to be cautious."

"What about my wife?" Geoff asked. "Can security be increased for her? She may be staying at the Capitol Plaza with her sister and niece."

"That's a good place. It employs a good security firm."

"Then perhaps I should stay there, as well."

"If you do please let us know, so we won't spend unnecessary time keeping watch on your house. Our patrolmen will keep a closer watch at the Capitol Plaza for the next few nights or until we get to the bottom of this situation."

"I'll be at the Capitol Plaza, then."

The man nodded, obviously satisfied that Geoff was willing to make his job easier.

"Does this mean you feel my wife and her family could be in danger?"

"I wouldn't say that, especially at this point, when we have no idea what happened. I just like to err on the side of caution."

He stood and shook Geoff's hand, ending the interview.

SEVEN

Fawn negotiated the bridge at Lake of the Ozarks with commendable expertise and had no trouble with the traffic surging around her. Even so, Karah Lee felt a growing need to get her hands on that steering wheel and rest her right foot on the comforting solidity of the real brake instead of the imaginary one she had been abusing on the drive up to Jefferson City.

Fawn gave her a sidelong glance. "I'm doing fine, you know. Are you amazed we haven't been in a wreck yet?"

"The word you're looking for is thankful. Not amazed, but thankful. Now, may I please drive? You've proven your skills, so I need to exercise mine. Jefferson City is unfamiliar to you. A wise driver—"

To her surprise, Fawn pulled to the side of the road and stopped. "You know what? You have a serious need to be in control, and I'm tired of worrying if you're going to scream at me about my next turn or stop. You drive."

"I don't scream at you."

"I probably have blisters on my ears."

For once, Karah Lee resisted the urge to snap back. She knew where all this emotion was coming from, and it wasn't fair to take it out on a stressed seventeen-year-old.

By the time she slid behind the steering wheel, Karah Lee was filled with remorse. "I'm sorry, okay? I'll try to be nicer the rest of the trip."

"Sure you'll be nicer now, you're back in control."

Karah Lee pulled back onto the dark road, stung by Fawn's words. "I don't always have to be in control."

"Yes, you do. You and Aunt Shona are a lot alike."

"That's a cruel thing to say."

Fawn laughed, breaking the tension. "That's why you two don't get along, because you're both always fighting for dominance."

"And you know that because?"

"Simple psychology. Plus I can't help overhearing your arguments."

"Those arguments aren't for teenaged ears."

"If you and Shona would realize what's going on, you'd get over yourselves long enough to become friends."

"You don't think we've tried?" Karah Lee asked. "We just clash." Divorce was so destructive, and their parents' divorce had split their family right down the middle.

Karah Lee knew she had exacerbated that split

between herself and her sister when, years ago, she abided by Mom's request not to tell Shona about Mom's cancer until it was too late for the two of them to make amends.

And now Dad was gone, and for the first time, Karah Lee could imagine how Shona must have felt all those years ago when Mom died with the situation still unsettled.

Karah Lee's eyes watered, and she questioned the wisdom of taking the wheel.

Shona sat in the busy ER waiting room feeling numb, trying hard not to think about anything at all. It amazed her that she had managed to remain unnoticed for the past ten minutes. To her relief, the press apparently had decided to leave after her announcement.

They must have expected her to leave. But where had they expected her to go?

Watching the door for Linda Plinkett's arrival, Shona choked back tears, swallowing hard to keep the pain at bay. The nightmare wouldn't end.

It was possible Linda had heard the news of Dad's passing and decided not to come to the hospital. That would be a relief.

Shona glanced at her watch for the third time in fifteen minutes. The policewoman should be on her way with a suitcase of clothing and cosmetics. The police didn't want Shona in the mansion. They had been adamant about it.

But why? An officer could have escorted her into her suite, kept watch over her all the time to make sure she didn't destroy evidence, then escorted her back out of the mansion.

Perhaps this way was best, though. Just closing her eyes and seeing the blood, seeing Dad's white face, was more than she felt able to handle right now.

She'd been asked to come up with names of people who had been in contact with him recently— friend or foe. That wouldn't be difficult. She had all her appointment and contact information on the electronic organizer in her purse. She called it her backup brain. Dad called the PDA—personal digital assistant—her baby.

But to suspect any of those people of murder? She couldn't do it.

An extremely overweight woman sank into the chair next to Shona's, overflowing beyond her seat, resting heavily against Shona's arm, her breathing labored.

"Did you hear the news?" the woman asked a man sitting across the aisle. "Somebody shot some important politician tonight."

"Just one?" The man snorted. "Should've gotten more while they had the bullets handy."

Shona's fingernails dug into the palms of her hands. She focused on keeping her face impassive. Long ago, she'd developed a tough hide about such comments, but tonight the man's attitude cut to the bone.

"I heard that announcement," another woman

said from the chair at the end of the row. "They didn't tell much. The guy was a state senator. My mother's best friend cleans the police station at night. She told my mother they think it was an inside job."

"How would you hear that so soon?" the man asked.

"My mother called to tell me about it just before my husband strained his back taking out the trash." The woman leaned toward them and lowered her voice. "You know the news guy on Channel 6? Geoff Tremaine? His wife was the senator's daughter." She nodded. "My mother's friend thinks the daughter did it."

The woman beside Shona shifted in her seat. "So the cleaning lady suddenly thinks she's judge and jury?"

"She told my mother they found a syringe rigged up like a booby trap in the Senator's fancy mansion. It was set up in a chair—probably his favorite one—so when he sat down, he got the full dose right in his—"

"Maybe you shouldn't be spreading tales like that," said Shona's armrest buddy. "That woman should be fired for spilling confidential information."

"Who better to know the senator's favorite chair than his daughter?" the man said, ignoring the reprimand.

The double glass doors of the waiting room opened. Shona glanced up to see her father's oldest and closest friend, Paul Forester, stepping inside. She rose quickly, excusing herself as she squeezed past her seatmate's arm and rushed to greet him in a corner of the room where they could have some privacy.

Though Paul looked hot and uncomfortable in his three-piece wool suit, he carried himself well, with broad straight shoulders. He had salt-and-pepper hair, cut military short, a gruff, bulldog face and bushy brows that gave the appearance of a man in control. Most of the time, he was.

"Uncle Paul, you heard?" Shona seldom used the childhood name for him anymore, but tonight she needed to.

He caught her in a bear hug and patted her shoulders briskly. "It's going to be okay, sweetheart." His gravelly voice comforted her. "Everything will be okay. I saw you and Geoff on the news just a few moments ago. I can't believe this is happening."

"They're treating it as a murder investigation."

"Has anyone said what happened?"

"I overheard a rumor just now and I intend to speak with a detective about it."

"You know what I think about rumors, my dear. Get the cold, hard facts or nothing at all."

"I do know what Dad told me when I found him." She repeated everything, whether it had made sense or not.

"Well, it's obvious to me he wanted you out of Jefferson City. That's the only possible deduction. As for the little one, he must have been hallucinating at that point. I think I'll go have a talk with that detective myself. Is he still around here?"

Shona relaxed a little. "I think he was talking with some of the medical personnel in one of the conference rooms."

Paul gave her another pat on the shoulder. "Linda's on her way, I believe. I know you'll want to see her."

Shona didn't reply, and she didn't respond to his astute glance. "Thanks, Paul. I'm glad you're here."

Geoff was standing on the sidewalk outside the hospital waiting room, arguing with Wendy Phillips on the telephone when Linda Plinkett drove into the parking lot.

"No, Wendy," he said into the phone, wishing he'd turned it off when he had a chance. "I didn't see Sally when we made the announcement. Didn't she tell you where she was going?"

Linda parked and got out quickly. Her usually perfect makeup was smudged, eyes red, her face puffy, and she wore a green silk jogging suit. Linda never went into the public eye unkempt. "Oh, honey," she said as she drew near, "where's Shona? I just heard."

"I need to get to work, Wendy." He disconnected, cutting his boss off mid-rant. He would pay for that later.

"She's inside," he said, accepting Linda's brief social hug.

"Is she doing okay?"

"She's pretty shaken up, but you know Shona. She'll handle it. Thank you for coming. I'm sure one of the detectives on the case will want to question you."

"I'd like to talk with Shona first," Linda said. "Paul's on his way here, the old blowhard. He's never happy unless he's in charge of things."

"He's already here. I saw him enter a few moments ago."

Linda frowned. "He probably came right in and took over."

On any other occasion, Geoff would have smiled at the evidence of open competition he had witnessed so many times between Linda and Paul.

"The newscaster suggested there might be some kind of foul play involved," Linda said. "What's this about a shooting?"

"There was no shooting."

"Then did Kemper have some kind of accident? What happened?"

"We don't know for sure yet, Linda." And if Shona had a better idea, she wasn't talking to reporters about it, even her estranged husband.

"Has the FBI been called in?" Linda asked.

"There have been rumors about that, but I'm not sure they would have jurisdiction in a case like this. Kemper was only a state senator. If the police do question you, would you have anything significant to tell them?"

Linda nodded. "I've been thinking about that on

my way here, though I was hoping it wouldn't come to that. You know, Kemper and Paul and I didn't always make everyone happy with our call for stiffer penalties against meth producers in the state, especially after Kemper joined the task force. We were also very vocal about the latest budget cuts. Many people were unhappy about that. We ruffled a lot of feathers."

"Do you think a drug kingpin might have decided to kill Kemper?"

"Not just any drug kingpin. Remember Beaufont Corporation and the run-in with your sister-in-law in Hideaway last year? I don't think those folks could be any too happy that Kemper pulled the feds down to check them out."

"Would they have killed him for it?"

"It's something to consider. Those people have their fingers in a lot of pies, some questionably legal. They wouldn't have thanked him for exposing them to the media barrage they received last year."

"They are probably also involved in meth production somewhere."

"Of course. That's the force behind a lot of the crime, simply because it brings in so much cash."

"Do you have names of any individuals for the police?"

Linda hesitated. "I'm sure the FBI will have more information than I would about Beaufont insiders. The agency keeps up with things like that. Besides, when an informant starts naming names in a police investigation, she'd better know what she's talking about or she can make a lot of enemies very quickly."

"So Beaufont is an organization the police would need to check out."

"The budget cuts might be another point of focus for the police," Linda continued, "though that would be such a wild card. Those cuts threaten to shut down a lot of programs people feel are necessary for life, even though many have been proven obsolete. Kemper told me just recently that his housekeeper's husband lost federal assistance for his epilepsy medication."

"But there are other medicines proven to work as well as or better than that particular drug, and they're still in the program."

Linda crossed her arms and leaned forward. "We don't know who might have grown angry enough about those cuts that they have decided to retaliate."

"So it could be anybody. But if Kemper was killed because of the drug task force, then you and Paul could also be in jeopardy."

"And Shona," Linda said softly. "I'm going to go have a talk with her." She patted Geoff's arm and headed for the entrance doors.

EIGHT

In spite of herself, Shona felt a quick rush of relief when she saw Linda Plinkett enter through the automatic sliding glass doors, looking disheveled and upset.

"Are you okay?" The older woman held her arms out, and Shona, by force of habit, stepped into them. Tears stung the backs of her lids. "I'll be fine."

Linda held her closely for a moment, then stepped back, holding Shona at arm's distance, studying her. "Can we go someplace and get some coffee?"

Shona led the way to a small private conference room along the hallway. There was a vending machine with hot drinks.

Linda selected black coffee, offered to buy Shona a cup, then took a seat at the table when Shona declined. "I want to hear about tonight. What happened?"

Shona sank into a chair across the table. "I'm not sure. It seems the police are keeping me in the dark about their discoveries."

"Well, why don't we have a talk with them and see

if we can teach them how to show some respect for—"

"I'll speak with them." Shona heard the cool tone in her voice and saw the flash of understanding in Linda's eyes. Linda wasn't going to take control of this situation. Shona wasn't going to allow it.

"I believe Dad was attacked from inside the house."

"How?"

"It's possible he received a deadly injection of some kind. Samples of his blood have been sent to a lab to be analyzed."

"So you're telling me someone Kemper knew— possibly someone we all knew—might have entered the house and murdered him?"

Shona nodded, feeling grief rip through her once again. Should she feel frightened? Somehow, she didn't seem to have enough emotional energy for that right now.

"But who could have done such a thing, Shona? Who has access?"

"It's a short list. I have access, Geoff still has access, Mrs. Reynolds, of course, you and Paul. I don't think Dad gave Jerrod a key or entry code, but I could be mistaken. The code hasn't been changed since Dad and Irene separated, so she may still have access."

"I told Kemper he should be more careful about who he gave keys to," Linda said. "Irene is long gone, and he needed to change pass codes. Your brother is a computer hacker. Depending on how knowledge-able, he might have been able to hack in. There's another person I would suspect if she had access, and that's Geoff's new boss."

"Dad would never have given Wendy Phillips access."

"True. She's the type to focus her destructive tendencies at him from the television, which she has done from time to time." Linda's expression softened, her brown eyes once more tearing. "I know Kemper was frustrated by that. He was also relieved to discover Geoff remained true to his word and didn't make a big deal on screen about his resignation. That resignation was a deep cut."

Shona studied Linda closely. She was a handsome woman with strong, even features and a tall, commanding presence. Shona guessed she was somewhere in her fifties, but she was one of those ageless beauties who defied time. In spite of the strength she portrayed, there was a feminine quality about her that she always played to her advantage. She could keep the attention of a room filled with argumentative politicians. Shona had never seen her cry, not during her divorce two years ago or even when her daughter, Kristin, then only fourteen, had chosen to live with her father rather than Linda.

"Shona? What is it?"

"Dad isn't…wasn't the type of man to wear his heart on his sleeve."

"I know that."

"And yet you seemed able to read him so…intimately."

Linda withdrew her elbows from the table and leaned back with a deep sigh. "I know there's been a problem between you and me. I hate that it turned out that way. I know this…this distance between us is because of my friendship and close working relationship with Kemper."

"That was more than a working relationship."

Linda winced. "I didn't intend for an affair to happen. I know it bothered you a great deal, which, in turn, disturbed me. Your father—" She shook her head. "He isn't easily rebuffed."

This wasn't something Shona wanted to hear. "Wasn't."

"Shona, I've never been so sorry about anything before in my life." Linda's deep, melodious voice offered warm comfort, which Shona refused to accept. "I realized, too late, after falling so hard for your father, that it had damaged our friendship. My motto has always been to never allow a man to come between girlfriends, because we need all the true friends we can get in this world. Especially in this business."

"This particular man had a wife."

Linda's expression froze over slightly. "This *particular* man had a marriage in name only. Irene was already separated from him, involved in a serious relationship with someone in Springfield, though few people knew about that at the time."

So that made everything okay? What about personal integrity? "What was your reaction when Dad broke off the relationship two weeks ago?" Shona asked.

Linda caught her gaze, and her eyes filled with sadness. "Why don't we get together sometime after the funeral and talk about that?" There was a hint of something in her voice…an unexpected gentleness that put Shona on guard.

"We have time now. The police haven't come with my things."

Linda looked away. "Things need to settle down a little. You need to get through a funeral and deal with your grief. There will be time later to discuss what happened."

Shona suddenly agreed. If Linda was going to deliver another revelation about Dad's past, Shona didn't want to hear it now. Maybe never.

"I've damaged our friendship," Linda said. "I'd love it if, when you've had some time to think about it, you'd give it another chance. The governor will most likely call you about filling Kemper's position as interim. I'd love to help with that, if you need it."

"I don't know. There hasn't been time to think." But Linda was right. Shona knew she was a natural choice to be her father's replacement, simply because she had knowledge about all his projects.

Somehow, though Shona realized business had to

continue, it felt inappropriate to be discussing this so soon after Dad's death.

Linda watched her in silence for a moment, then sighed and reached across the table. Her fingers stopped just short of Shona's hand. "Your father often struggled because he couldn't seem to live up to his own expectations. The pressure was one reason he sometimes drank too much. Guilt can do that to people."

"I know he felt a lot of self-recrimination," Shona said. That had been the one thing, in the past couple of weeks, that had caused her to doubt her decision to resign. Dad had seemed so regretful about their fight and the events that led up to it.

Linda paused for a moment, then asked hesitantly, "Is it possible your father did this to himself?"

Shona recoiled, startled. "You're saying you think he brought this on? He deserved to die?"

"No, of course not. I'm saying maybe he wanted to die."

Surprise became horror. "You think Dad committed suicide?"

"I'm only asking if you think it might be a possibility."

"Of course not!"

Linda watched her and said nothing.

"How can you even suggest such a thing?"

"We're looking for reasons for his death. I'm simply presenting a possibility."

"Dad would never do that."

Linda closed her eyes and sighed. "You might be surprised by some of the things your father would have done."

Shona pushed her chair back and stood. "If you'll excuse me, I need to see a detective about a murder."

NINE

Geoff tried Shona's cell phone and was transferred to her answering service. He didn't want to leave the hospital until he spoke with her one more time, if she would talk with him.

He left a message, asking her to call him as soon as possible. She needed to understand the seriousness of her situation. Right now, she was so overwhelmed with her loss, he doubted she would comprehend the need to be cautious or that the police could convey that danger to her adequately. She was a tenacious woman, rarely daunted.

In the past months, since their separation, he discovered he had more than tenacity—he had spiritual strength from the faith of his youth. Somewhere along the way, he had lost that first glow of faith in Christ, but apparently the Spirit of Christ had never left him.

He'd turned to God during the dark days immediately after he quit his job and he and Shona had parted. During that time, he was more depressed and discouraged than any other period of his life. And yet, it was then that he had found the most hope.

Shona needed that hope.

He stepped outside into the late spring evening and punched Karah Lee's number in his cell phone.

Fawn answered almost immediately. "Hi, Uncle Geoff."

"Did Karah Lee finally beat you away from the steering wheel?"

"No, I just gave up the fight. Karah Lee, watch it, you're crossing the line. Dim your lights, there's a car coming."

Geoff had never had the pleasure of meeting the teenager who had captured his sister-in-law's heart, but he'd spoken with her over the phone several times. Karah Lee had always treated him as a brother, maintaining contact even after he and Shona had separated.

"How far are you from Jeff?" he asked Fawn.

"Maybe an hour," she said. "Or more, slow as Karah Lee drives."

"Have you managed to contact Shona?"

"No, we tried, but her phone's off or something. Karah Lee reserved a suite at the Capitol Plaza, just in case, and it's got two bedrooms and a sleeper sofa in the living room. Guess who gets the sofa?"

"I'll tell you what. I'll go home, pack, and reserve a room for myself at the same hotel. We'll both keep trying to reach Shona to tell her our plans. When she discovers we've all decided to stay at the Capitol

Plaza, she's likely to change her mind just because she's so obstinate."

"Just like Karah Lee," Fawn said. "Any leads on what happened?"

Geoff closed his eyes. "There are a lot of rumors already flying around. Will you let me talk to Karah Lee?"

"Sure, but she isn't in a very good mood."

"I'll risk it."

Karah Lee's voice came over the line. She sounded tired, her voice was hoarse—most likely from nagging Fawn about driving too fast. "What's up?"

"I need to know how much you know about your brother. Remember the first time he arrived in Hideaway and hacked into the files?"

"It isn't as if I'm going to forget that very soon."

"Were those just your personnel files, or did he attempt to hack into your medical files, as well?"

Karah Lee's curiosity could be felt in the silence over the line.

"I don't know if it means anything," Geoff said. "But I just wanted to know."

"He told me it was my personnel files."

"You're sure about that? Was there any follow-up investigation?"

"Nope. After he introduced himself and proved who he was, we understood that he'd wanted to be sure I was his sister so he wouldn't make a fool of himself when he *did* introduce himself."

"Are you absolutely confident about that?"

There was another silence, and this time Geoff could sense Karah Lee's alarm. He regretted doing this, because she didn't need any more stress or fear tonight. Her estranged father had just died. She didn't know what to expect when she arrived in Jefferson City. And now her newfound brother might be a suspect.

"Mind telling me where you're getting these questions?" she asked.

"The detective who interviewed me mentioned that Jerrod had hacked into your medical files and Shona's and your father's."

"Where would he hear something like that?"

"Good question, especially this early in the investigation, unless the police had some kind of file on Jerrod already. Is it possible he found a way into your medical files?" Geoff asked.

"I don't want to think so, but I don't know. I'm not a computer expert."

"Did anyone do a background check on him after your father decided to accept him into the fold?"

"Of course. I'm engaged to a forest ranger, remember? That's comparable to the police in our town. Taylor couldn't just let it go. He checked it out, and Jerrod's story matched his background. Why would Jerrod need to check our medical files?"

"I don't know, but in light of the investigation, I think someone should try to find out," Geoff said.

"Who do you know in Hideaway who can track Jerrod's movements on the computer?"

"After all this time? Is that possible?"

"Sure it is."

Karah Lee sighed. "I'll call Taylor. There's a deputy in town who lives on the computer. He may be able to do some checking."

"Good. I'm sorry to have to do this, but—"

"I know. There's a murder investigation afoot," Karah Lee said. "This kind of thing seems to be following my family this past year."

"I know it seems that way."

"I'm doing some heavy praying right now, but I don't know what else I can do."

"Pray for Shona while you're at it, will you?"

"We're already doing that."

"Thanks. I'll see you in a while." He disconnected, and decided he needed to do some praying himself.

The dew-laden evening enveloped Shona as she stepped out the exit door. She inhaled the scent of damp concrete mingled with the aroma of the abundant flowers that surrounded the hospital.

Detective Milt Davis stood in the parking lot, talking quietly with Officer Marsh, who had brought Shona a suitcase from the mansion.

"May I speak with you for a few moments, Milt?" Shona asked.

"Have you thought of something else?"

She walked a few steps away and was relieved when he followed her. She didn't want anyone else in this discussion until she knew more. "We know my father wasn't shot, but I think he was trying to tell me he had *received* a shot. Isn't that right?"

"You've spoken with the doctor?"

"This information didn't come from the doctor, it came from the police station. I think it's interesting that police station ancillary staff and strangers in the hospital waiting room know more about my father's murder investigation than I do. Would it have been so hard for someone to tell me about the syringe that was found in my father's chair?" She heard the tremor in her voice.

"I'm sorry," the detective said gently. "You know how rumors can fly at times like this."

"So it's just a rumor? Or did my father receive an injection of some kind that killed him?"

He sighed. "It's possible."

"*Was* a syringe found?"

"There were actually three syringes found in his office chair, apparently inserted into the cushion in a way that would insure the injections of a considerable amount of fluid. The lab is checking the residue now."

"Could it have been blood thinner?"

"We suspect that, but we can't be sure until the results return from the lab. What doesn't make sense is the fact that a blood thinner would take considerable time to do its damage, according to the doctors, it could take hours, even at a high dosage. We can't figure out why he wouldn't have called for help during that time."

"He wouldn't call for help if he didn't realize he needed it. If the chair was rigged to inject him, he could have thought a spring had broken, but he would have checked. That still leaves unanswered questions."

The detective nodded. "We still need to know who had access to the house."

She held up her purse, which she had retrieved earlier from her car. "I have a PDA with information on everyone who might have had that access." Now, with her laptop still being held hostage at the house, she was glad she had her backup brain to help her with the investigation.

"Does that thing have phone numbers and addresses for office and household staff?"

"That's correct, and everything's up-to-date. I synchronize this with my desktop computer often."

"Did the housekeeper always agree with your father's politics?" the detective asked.

"No."

"Has there been any change in their relationship recently?"

Shona hesitated. "They've never interacted much. Mrs. Reynolds has been more reserved in the past few weeks, but I didn't notice anything unusual. I know she wasn't happy about the budget cuts that affected her husband's medication. That isn't something for which one would commit murder."

"You might be surprised what could take place in the mind of a murderer. How about your husband? Would he have any reason to hurt your father?"

"My husband is not a murderer."

"People can surprise you. What was it your father told you when you found him? Do you think it's possible he was warning you to get away from your husband?"

"As I've explained already, I wasn't thinking about anything except getting help for Dad. His comments never registered, and parts of them made no sense. He might have simply been hallucinating."

"Shona, because we were aware of your father's run-in with the Beaufont Corporation in Hideaway last year, and because of possible ties between Beaufont and organized crime in the state, the FBI has been consulted about your father's death. We found the FBI has a few interesting items on file, the most important at this moment, I believe, being the fact that someone hacked into your father's, your sister's and your medical files some months ago."

"For what?"

"That's what we're trying to uncover. Does your father have any drug allergies of any kind? Perhaps something that could have caused the response that took his life tonight?"

"You're saying someone might have been searching for a specific allergen in order to personalize Dad's death?" This was becoming too bizarre...and too frightening.

"We know your brother once hacked into your sister's personnel file and some of the electronic signatures are the same."

"How do you know that?"

"Your father had a run-in with a known crime syndicate in the past year. The FBI watches for possible backlashes when something like that occurs."

Shona's hands began trembling. In fact, her whole body was trembling. Tears burned her eyes. She tamped down on her grief once more. There would be time for it later. Right now, she had to do everything possible to help the police find her father's killer.

"Why don't you show me what you have on your little computer," Milt suggested. "I need some more people to interview. Believe me, we've got all available staff on this case. We've even pulled personnel from other cases to help us. We're going to get to the bottom of this."

It was 10:15 p.m. when Karah Lee pulled into the parking lot of the Capitol Plaza Hotel. Fawn had finally managed to reach Shona, and she was to meet them here.

"I still think she should have met us somewhere else and ridden with us," Fawn said. "She wants to avoid the press, right? That big SUV of hers is a motorized advertisement."

"You made the mistake of telling her that." Karah Lee got out and reached into the backseat for the overnight case she'd packed in less than five minutes. "Never try to tell her anything."

"You're starting it again," Fawn warned. "Be nice."

"Sorry. Shona likes her mobility. You'll never see her dependent on anyone for anything."

"You know what they say about that *never* word." Fawn grabbed her own backpack, locked the door and joined Karah Lee. "It's daring God to prove you wrong."

Karah Lee placed an arm over the girl's shoulder and pointed toward the white Cadillac Escalade cruising toward them. "Looks like our timing is good."

Fawn rushed forward as Shona parked.

Karah Lee's heart beat a little faster. That was what Shona did to her. Always, there was tension. When they were growing up, Karah Lee had idolized her older sister. Shona was active in school politics, sports, the National Honor Society and she'd been the valedictorian of her class.

Karah Lee had to study to keep her grades high, whereas Shona seemed able to cruise through school with little difficulty. Karah Lee had always felt like a disappointment to her parents and her teachers in comparison to her sister.

When Mom and Dad divorced and Shona sided

with Dad, Karah Lee had been devastated. Their relationship had gone downhill from that point. How was it a teenager like Fawn could charm them both?

Fawn flung herself into Shona's arms, hugging her with the same exuberance with which she hugged Karah Lee. Looking on, Karah Lee pushed back a shameful shroud of jealousy that threatened to smother her as she followed Fawn. She was as sure of a brush-off from her sister as she was that, for some reason, she must deserve it.

Shona clung to Fawn, eyes squeezed shut tight, obviously struggling against a flood of emotions. Karah Lee found herself battling those same emotions.

Their roles were reversed this time. Years ago, Shona had been the one on the outside looking in at Karah Lee's grief after Mom's death.

Losing Dad was a shock, and Shona would be the one who took the hit the hardest.

"You doing okay?" came Fawn's muffled voice from the folds of Shona's jacket.

Shona released her. "I'll be fine, honey." Almost reluctantly, she looked at Karah Lee. "Hi."

"Hi."

"I'm glad you came," Shona said.

Karah Lee didn't believe her, but this was still the right thing to do. "We've booked a suite, two bedrooms, so you won't have to talk to anyone if you don't want to."

"I'm suddenly not in the mood to stay alone."

Shona pulled a leather case from the backseat of her SUV, slung her purse over her shoulder and gave Karah Lee a glance. "I wasn't going to call you."

"I didn't think you would have."

"But Geoff did the right thing."

"He always does. Can you leave town after the funeral for a few days? You could come back to Hideaway with us." Oh, sure, like that was going to happen. Still, the invitation needed to be placed on the table.

Shona hesitated for a moment, as if she might actually be considering it. Amazing. Then she shook her head. "I have too much work to do. The staff will need some direction, and if I'm appointed to step into Dad's position as interim, I need to be prepared."

"You can't even get into the mansion right now," Karah Lee said. "It's a crime scene."

"I have my PDA and, according to you, a suite here at the hotel. That's enough for now."

Karah Lee followed her into the lobby.

Shona hesitated inside the door, her dark eyes wide and apprehensive, and then sudden tears filled those eyes and spilled down her cheeks.

Karah Lee touched her shoulder. "It's going to be okay," she said softly.

Shona's chin wobbled. She turned as if to speak, then her gaze shifted toward the entrance. The tears dried, the chin grew firm, the eyes narrowed.

Karah Lee turned to find her brother-in-law

walking through the door with a duffel bag slung over his shoulder.

As Shona went to the desk to check in, Geoff stepped up to Karah Lee. "Did you call Taylor?"

"Yes. You know Blaze Farmer? He lives at the boys' ranch across the lake. He attends College of the Ozarks, and he's good friends with Fawn."

"Yes. Smart kid. Doesn't he work with you?"

"When he gets a chance," Karah Lee said. "He's taken some computer courses and has a special affinity for them. He did some preliminary checking and called me. He thinks it looks as if someone might have hacked into the medical files, then tried to cover their tracks. Fawn spoke with him a few minutes ago."

"Does he think it was Jerrod?"

Karah Lee gave a casual shrug, though she felt anything but casual. This was her brother they were talking about. True, she had only recently made his acquaintance, but it would still be hard to take—and it would wound Shona—if they discovered Jerrod might have had something to do with their father's death.

Karah Lee had been the one to insist Dad meet Jerrod.

"Taylor is calling in a computer expert from Springfield," she said. "He'll contact me as soon as they find anything out for sure."

First, she had asked Dad to help her with the Beaufont crisis in Hideaway, then she had insisted

Dad meet with Jerrod. It was looking more and more possible that she could have been instrumental in her father's death.

TEN

Early Saturday morning, Shona sat on the back deck of the hotel suite, soaking up the sun and trying not to cough as cigarette smoke drifted up from the deck below. She couldn't help listening through the door as Karah Lee and Fawn argued over what kind of flowers to order for the funeral. Then the subject switched to the upcoming wedding.

Karah Lee was truly in love. Just listening to her gave Shona a pang. It was difficult to remember when she and Geoff had shared that quality of rapport.

She could credit Geoff with the once-upon-a-time strength of their marriage. She grudgingly took partial blame for its failure.

The glass door rumbled open and Karah Lee came out carrying two mugs. She handed one to Shona and settled into the chair beside her.

"Decaf?" Shona asked, remembering Geoff's advice in the hospital waiting room.

"Even worse. It's a coffee substitute I brought

from Noelle's Naturals in Hideaway. Don't turn your nose up like that until you've tasted it."

Shona sipped, nodded politely, and resisted the urge to spit it over the side of the deck. The guy smoking his cigarette on the deck below wouldn't thank her for that.

"So you're on a health kick?" she asked her younger sister. "You look like you've lost a few pounds."

"Thirty-one and three-quarters, but who's counting?" Karah Lee leaned back and rested her feet on the deck rail. "Tell me about Linda Trinket."

"Plinkett."

"Whatever. Didn't you tell me once she was the siren of the Capitol Building?"

Shona gave her a sharp look, pressing her forefinger against her lips, then pointing downward, from whence the smoke continued to drift. She picked up her mug—though she would have preferred to leave it out there—and gestured for Karah Lee to follow her inside.

"Don't ever get into politics," she said after sliding the glass door behind her. "You don't think before you speak."

"Sorry. You're absolutely right." Sarcasm underlined every word. "I'll have to reconsider my bid for the presidency. Was Linda the siren—"

"Let's just say I've always thought she was very good at getting what she wanted, and she's a beautiful woman."

"Wasn't she a friend of yours?"

Shona took her time placing her mug on the kitchenette counter. "I thought she was."

"What happened?"

"She…and Dad…"

Karah Lee choked on her drink and put her mug on the counter beside Shona's. "She had an affair with Dad?"

Shona sighed. She was tired of defending their father's memory. She was also tired of thinking about his past indiscretions. Jerrod was reminder enough.

"How long did that go on?" Karah Lee asked.

"Until a couple of weeks ago."

"You're kidding! Did Linda dump him?"

"I don't know for sure what happened. I noticed a definite chill between them recently whenever they crossed paths. Dad and I were supposed to meet Linda, Paul and their staff at a dinner last night, and I knew Dad wasn't looking forward to it."

"Did you ask him what happened between them?"

"How could I when he never even acknowledged the affair in the first place? And besides, I wasn't speaking to him much, either."

"Okay, but he's dead now, and it looks very much like murder. Don't you think you need to check out a little more about his relationship with Linda?"

"I spoke with her last night, and I don't think she'll be very forthcoming with me. She's very astute. She isn't going to incriminate herself."

"You could try again."

"There are policemen to do that." Shona hated the prospect of further conversation with Linda Plinkett.

"She won't tell the police any more than she'll tell you," Karah Lee pointed out. "At least with you, she might let her guard down. If she's been that close to Dad, working with him on that drug committee, the two of you together might be able to reach the bottom of this."

"If she knows anything, she'll tell the police."

Karah Lee leaned back on the counter. "What is it about her that scares you?"

"I'm not afraid of her," Shona snapped.

"Oh, yes, you are. You're afraid if you confront her it'll be political suicide."

"That's ridiculous. How can you say that?"

"Hey!" came Fawn's voice through the bathroom door. "Don't make me come out there!"

Shona held Karah Lee's stare for a few seconds, then broke the connection and turned away. "We're talking about Dad's murderer, here, Karah Lee. You really think I would place my own political agenda— which I don't even have, by the way—ahead of finding the killer?"

"Then what's stopping you from talking to Linda again?"

"I just spoke with her last night. I didn't get anywhere. I think there's something she isn't telling me, but she wouldn't say more. All she said was that she thought Dad might have killed himself."

Karah Lee gasped. "You know he wouldn't do that."

"I didn't argue with her."

"Are you afraid of what else she might tell you?" Karah Lee asked softly.

Shona started to protest, but she couldn't.

"You think Linda knows something else about Dad's activities—"

"Stop it." Shona heard a warning thump on the bathroom door and lowered her voice. "Just stop it, okay? You've always been so quick to believe the worst of him. He wasn't an ogre, you know. But then, how could you know? You never made any effort to get to know him and see his heart—see the reason behind so many of the decisions he made."

"Then why don't you try to explain it to me." Karah Lee, too, kept her voice down.

"Dad always had this…this passion for Missouri. He honestly couldn't believe anyone could love this state as much as he did, and so he took steps to make sure he would be in the best position to control what happened here."

"He wanted to be governor, didn't he?"

"Yes."

"If anyone had found out about his affair with Linda, that would have been a scandal for him," Karah Lee said. "And so he broke it off. But what if Linda didn't take that well?"

"That's ridiculous. She's one of the most powerful women in the state, and she got there with a level head and good priorities."

"And good looks. Don't forget that."

"She isn't going to blow it all by killing a man for ending their relationship."

"I'll talk to her. Maybe I can—"

"She relates better to men," Shona said. "She seems to have this...this power over them. I've seen men, from twenty to ninety, following her around like lovelorn teenagers. She's come to expect it."

"How about having Paul talk to her?" Karah Lee asked. "She works with him on the committee."

"Mmm." Shona thought for a moment, then said, "How about Geoff? I know Linda admires him, and she's always found him attractive. I've heard her accuse Paul of being an annoying rule-follower."

"Geoff is a rule-follower," Karah Lee said.

"But Linda definitely doesn't find him annoying."

"And he's a man. What makes you think he won't be susceptible to Linda?"

"He's very discerning," Shona said. "And he's never appreciated her lifestyle. Besides, she's more likely to talk to him than me, simply because she doesn't think he can see through her. She knows me well enough to realize I can."

"Do you think Geoff's gone to work yet this morning?"

"How should I know?" Shona asked. "It isn't as if I'm part of his life now."

Karah Lee pulled her cell phone from her pocket and held it out to Shona. "This one's on me. Call Geoff."

Shona shook her head. She wasn't up to talking to him this early in the morning. "You call. Just tell him what you told me. He knows Dad's history with Linda. It was one of the reasons he quit."

Geoff checked his buzzing cell phone as he walked into the station, and saw that the caller was Karah Lee. He answered. "Hey. What's up with you this early?"

"Shona and I have an assignment for you, should you choose to accept it."

He glanced up and down the long hallway and saw Wendy striding from the administration office. "Oh, boy, sounds serious. An assignment doing what?"

"All you need to do is take a certain lady out to dinner and have a little talk with her."

He waved at Wendy as he passed her in the wide corridor. No daggers shot from her eyes, so he was safe for now. Never could tell with her. "Are you matchmaking, Karah Lee?" he teased softly.

"Certainly not. If I were matchmaking I would make sure the lady was my sister."

He frowned. "It isn't?"

"Not even close. We'd like you to give Linda Trinket a call."

"Plinkett," came Shona's voice in the background.

"Her name is Plinkett, Karah Lee. Why can't you remember that?"

"Why do you want me to call Linda?" Geoff asked.

"We need to know more about her relationship with Kemper before he died," Karah Lee said. "Specifically, we need to know why their relationship suddenly grew chilly about two weeks ago."

"I already know why."

"Really? Why? And why didn't you tell us?"

Geoff sighed. "I was waiting for Kemper to talk to you himself. It wasn't my place."

"It is now," Karah Lee said quietly.

"Your father became a Christian just about two weeks ago," Geoff said. "He came to my house and spoke with me about it. I didn't tell Shona last night because there were a lot of other things on her mind, and she most likely wouldn't have appreciated it, anyway. She tends to hold with her father's belief system. Or rather, his former belief system."

"Did you tell the police?"

"Yes, I spoke to Shona's detective, Milt Davis last night. He didn't seem to think that would have any impact on the investigation."

"Wow," Karah Lee said softly.

"What?" Shona asked in the background. "What are you two talking about?"

"Karah Lee, tell Shona I'll talk to her about it later. I firmly believe that Kemper broke off the relationship because he wanted to do the right thing."

"Fine, I'll tell her, but meanwhile, will you place a friendly call to Linda and ask her to meet you for dinner?"

"I don't want to take Linda to dinner. Don't you have something else I could do? You know, like water the trees around the mansion? Linda isn't going to kill a man just because he broke off a relationship."

"Well, okay then, it sounds as if you've already solved the case," came Karah Lee's sarcastic reply. "Who's the lucky winner?"

"Karah Lee, stop that," came Shona's warning in the background.

"Sorry," Karah Lee muttered. "Just talk to Linda, okay, Geoff? Old times sake? You know how to do these things. Get her to let her hair down. You're good-looking, she'll be susceptible to you if she was susceptible to my old dad."

Geoff couldn't believe what his sister-in-law was suggesting. And he couldn't believe his wife was supporting her. Had he suddenly entered a world of spies and espionage?

"No, Karah Lee, I'm not the kind of—"

"You'd rather allow the police—who don't know Linda or the situation as well as you do—to continue the difficult investigation by themselves? They already have their hands full."

"Has Shona not warned you that I don't cave to MacDonald family manipulations?"

"Please, Geoff? Just a little talk, to get some details.

In the meantime, we'll be working on the Jerrod angle."

"The Jerrod angle? Did you find something more?"

"I haven't heard from Taylor yet this morning, but Jerrod apparently had more contact with Dad than we had realized, judging by this copy of Dad's telephone bill we managed to have faxed to us this morning from the phone company."

"You really think he's a suspect?"

"Can't be too careful. We're also checking out Mrs. Reynolds, not because Shona thinks she could be guilty, but simply because her husband works for a veterinarian and has access to drugs that could have caused Dad's reaction last night." Her voice softened, and he could hear the sadness break through. "I'm even checking with some people in Jefferson City who did some work for Dad a couple of months ago. It isn't as if we're sitting on our thumbs here. We're doing our share. You could help."

In the background, he could hear Shona speaking. "Karah Lee, you talk to him like that you're not going to get any help from him!"

He closed his eyes and sighed. His wife still knew him well. "Okay, I'll do it."

"That's what I thought. Get a date with her and find out what you can."

"It will be a pleasure."

There was a pause, then: "What's that supposed to mean?"

He chuckled wickedly and ended the call.

* * *

Karah Lee slumped onto the sofa beside her sister, who was thumbing through a photo book of floral arrangements for funerals.

"I knew he'd do it for you," Shona said.

Karah Lee peered at the arrangements. They all looked so…funeral. "He'd have done it for you, but you're suddenly such a coward. What's going on with you, anyway?"

Shona didn't reply for a moment, but continued to stare at the page. "Have you ever done anything that you later deeply regretted?"

"Plenty of things."

"For instance?"

Karah Lee sat back, crossing her legs beneath her. "I'll always regret that Dad and I didn't have a closer relationship."

"Dad had as much to do with that as you did."

Karah Lee gave her an exaggerated look of surprise. "I can't believe you just said that. You've always been his champion."

"He's always needed one. I saw how much it hurt him when you took Mom's side, and I've seen, over the years, how much he's messed up his own relationships. He needed someone to be loyal."

"You're saying I wasn't loyal?"

"No, that's not what I'm saying."

"I was loyal to Mom."

"So there you go. You took Mom's side, I stayed with Dad."

"Were you ever sorry?" Karah Lee asked.

"What do you think? I didn't speak to Mom for a whole year and then I found out she was dying of cancer. And you didn't tell me."

"She wouldn't let me."

"Well, you should have, anyway."

"And break the trust of a dying woman?"

Shona sighed, leaning her head against the back of the sofa. "That's a regret I'll always have. Mom didn't live long enough for us to completely reconcile, or at least, not long enough for me to make up for the years I avoided her because of the bitterness of the divorce."

"I'm worried about you," Karah Lee said.

Shona looked up at her sister. "Hmm?"

"We've fought almost constantly for years. Now, all of a sudden, you seem different. You're not as… contentious."

Shona turned a page and studied another arrangement. "I guess shock and grief do strange things to some people."

Karah Lee heard the sarcasm in Shona's voice. They had both been especially gifted with that quality.

"I noticed Geoff was by your side as soon as he could get there last night," Karah Lee said.

Someone knocked at the door, and Shona turned quickly to answer, most likely grateful for the interruption.

ELEVEN

Shona's relief was short-lived. She opened the door to find Detective Milt Davis standing in the hallway. Officer Marsh, the woman who had packed Shona's suitcase, stood beside him. Both looked grim.

"Mrs. Tremaine," Milt said, more formal than he had been last night. "Could we speak with you for a few moments in private?"

"Sure." She stepped back to allow them inside. "My sister and niece are—"

"Fawn and I are on our way downstairs for breakfast," Karah Lee informed them as she breezed toward the door, Fawn in tow. "I'll be on my cell phone, Shona. Call me if you need anything. There's some coffee left if anyone wants a cup."

Shona watched them leave, feeling suddenly ill at ease. She led the way to the living room sofa and chairs. "I should warn you that stuff in the pot is not coffee. It's some herbal brew my sister brought with her from Hideaway."

"Thanks for the warning," Milt said. "There's a new Starbucks not far from here. We'll stop by there in a few minutes."

Good. That meant they didn't plan to stay long. "Have you received the results of my dad's blood tests?" Shona asked.

"No, but we've heard from the lab in Columbia about the three syringes that were found in his chair. The residue was injectable Coumadin, heparin and Versed. The first two are blood thinners, and Versed is a fast-acting tranquilizer. The way it was explained to us, the thinners would have combined to wipe out all your father's clotting factors, and Versed would have kept him immobile long enough for him to bleed to death. He wouldn't have had time to call for help."

"But he had apparently been in the dining room and kitchen not long before I found him. The blood was still fresh."

"We figure he must have awakened and gone in search of his cordless telephone."

The horror of her father's murder struck Shona afresh, but she refused to show emotion in front of the police.

"Mrs. Tremaine—"

"Milt, I thought we had decided on first names," she said. "What's changed since last night?"

The police officers shared a brief glance.

"What's happened?"

Milt cleared his throat. "You and your father were

overheard arguing two weeks ago in his office at the Capitol Building." He said the words with reluctance.

"I know. I'm ashamed of that."

"Your voices grew loud enough that people walking past the closed door could hear parts of the conversation. Would you care to tell me what that was about?"

"It was no secret that my father and I were having a few disagreements. I had just discovered he'd decided to change his vote on the legalized gambling issue after promising his constituents he would not support it." All those trusting little elderly ladies who sent him their extra spending money for his war chest...

"Mrs. Tremaine, did the senator threaten to demote you if you continued to disregard his orders?"

"What he said was, 'I'm going to change your job title if you keep nagging me.' That's a favorite—or rather, it *was* a favorite warning of his—every time we had an argument."

"Did you have those often?"

"Not often in public, as that one was," she said.

He hesitated, sighed, continued. "Do you have access to medical or veterinarian supplies, particularly drugs such as Heparin, Coumadin or Versed?"

"Why would I have access to those substances? I'm a senator's aide and assistant, not a doctor or nurse."

"Your sister is a doctor, is she not?"

"Karah Lee? Well, yes, but it isn't as if she's going to give me free access to—"

"A neighbor observed you entering the house around two o'clock yesterday afternoon, then leaving quickly," Officer Marsh said. "Can you tell us what you were doing there at that time?"

"Of course. I had left some briefs for a meeting in my room by mistake and had to return home and get them." If only she had gone into Dad's office then. If only he hadn't given the staff Friday afternoons off.

"We need to take a set of fingerprints from you to distinguish your prints from anyone else's who might have been there," Officer Marsh said.

Shona held out her hands. "You can take my prints anytime, if this will help us find Dad's killer, but you'll find prints from many people in that office."

"If you would stop by the station sometime this morning," Milt said, "we'll leave word for them to take the prints as discreetly as possible."

"So does this mean I'm on the suspect list?" This couldn't be happening. How could anyone suspect her of murder?

Another quick glance shot between Milt and his partner. "We have a lot of suspects right now, Shona," Milt said. "We're checking everything and everyone."

"I understand."

"Can you tell me why your father might have visited your husband the day after your big fight at the Capitol Building?"

If the man had intended to startle her, he had certainly succeeded. However, long ingrained control of her facial features gave her the upper hand in this interview…for now.

"Is there some reason why my father shouldn't have spoken to my husband at that time? It wasn't as if they were estranged. Geoff is separated from me, not from my family."

"Wasn't your husband's anger over your father's politics the main wedge between the two of you?"

"Even if it were, that isn't going to keep people from talking in this town. Business must go on as usual. My father and my husband were capable of moving beyond their differences."

"What kind of business would they have had with one another?" Officer Marsh asked.

"I have no idea. I was my father's daughter, aide and assistant, but I wasn't always his confidante. If you want to know about that conversation, you'll have to ask Geoff."

"That's what we plan to do," Milt said. "Is there anything you can tell us about your stepmother, Irene Tremaine?"

"I haven't seen her for weeks. I understand she's in Springfield at this time, and I haven't called her about Dad."

Milt's eyebrows rose.

"They've been separated for a year," Shona explained.

He hesitated long enough to digest this information and jot something down in his notebook. "Do you know if she's a beneficiary in his will or a life insurance policy?"

"If you're looking for motive for Irene, she and Dad had a prenuptial agreement, and all of Dad's assets before the marriage were placed in a living trust. He changed his life insurance beneficiaries when they separated." Though Shona and Irene hadn't always gotten along, Shona felt sorry for her. Irene was not cut out to be the wife of a politician. Shona believed Irene, to her credit, really had loved Kemper at one time, however briefly.

Milt closed his notebook and stood. "Thank you, Shona. I'll call the station as soon as we leave, and they'll be prepared for you when you arrive."

Geoff sat in front of his dressing room mirror and studied the circles beneath his eyes. "Must the show always go on?" he muttered to his reflection.

He would have asked for the day off, but he didn't have seniority. Wendy would complain.

He had stayed up until the early hours this morning talking to Karah Lee and Fawn at the hotel after Shona went to bed. He'd been able to pick up on Shona's tension all the way across the room— which was as close as she would allow him to get to her. Though she had let her guard down for a short while at the hospital, that guard had aggressively re-asserted itself.

Shona Tremaine had always had a tender spot

when it came to her sister—tender to the point of pain over their long-term rift. On occasion, she avoided Karah Lee altogether in order to elude another hurtful fight with her. Shona had always been able to get along very well with people when it didn't affect her heart. For those few who got past her emotional defenses, she was hypersensitive and easily wounded. Karah Lee, for all her intelligence, had never understood that. Geoff had.

And now, Shona was treating him the way she had always treated Karah Lee.

There was a brisk knock at the closed door of his dressing room. When he opened it, a storm named Wendy Phillips burst inside, a thundercloud on her face, her eyes shooting fire.

She sank into the plush recliner he kept in the room for the odd hour when he wasn't frantic with work. "We've got a problem, Tremaine, and I need to know if you're going to work with me on this, or if we're going to butt heads."

"I'm sorry?"

"You sent a crew away last night from one of the hottest events we've covered in months, after you had specifically coaxed me into allowing you to remain at the hospital to be the first with news from your wife."

"I did not send the crew away, I simply told them the family was not yet ready to make a statement. I didn't have any information to share, and Shona was still struggling with the tragedy. We both gave a statement later, but by then Sally had already left."

"Are you trying to shut this station out of the ratings altogether?"

He glared at her. Hadn't she even heard what he just said?

"I've spoken with Sally," she said. "She told me she had a very important event to attend with her husband last night, one she couldn't afford to miss. She's on probation. Right now we're focusing on *your* part in this."

"I was trying to comfort my wife through a horrible situation."

"Oh, come on. You and Shona are getting a divorce, and yet you're going all protective of her. Man, we have a show to produce! We needed that interview last night that you refused to give."

"I didn't refuse. I didn't know anything at that point except that Shona needed my support. There's no good reason to neglect human compassion in favor of ratings."

Wendy's expression chilled and hardened. "I'm a professional with a job to do. That job is covering the news in this city. You're an employee of this station. You could have a little loyalty to the company that took you in when you didn't have a job."

Geoff studied the heightened color in her face, the snap of anger in her pretty eyes, and decided not to argue. He'd said enough already.

"There are plenty of others willing and waiting to take your place," she said.

"I'm sure that's true, as you've reminded me on several occasions. You have my blessing if you choose to replace me." At this point, he was ready to quit. The only thing keeping him here, beside his need for employment, was his desire to serve as a buffer between Shona and Wendy.

His hiring, which had probably happened only because of Wendy's grudge against Kemper, had turned into a good choice, according to the viewing audience. Geoff had often thanked God for it.

He knew Wendy wouldn't hesitate to fire him when he no longer had use for him. In fact, he had been contacted by a rival station in Columbia more than once to work for them. Wendy knew about it. Columbia was only thirty minutes away, and he'd thought about accepting the offer several times.

"Let me tell you about a perfect way to make this up to me," she said, her voice softening.

"I'm not convinced I've done anything for which I need to make reparation."

She gestured to the floor. "You don't see that thin ice beneath your feet? Convince Shona to give us an exclusive interview."

"I can tell you right now that won't happen. She has a memory, Wendy. You've cast too many aspersions on the MacDonald—"

"How far would she go to save your job?"

"My job is not her problem."

"Fine, then if she won't do it to save your job, would she do it to save her reputation in this state?"

"Why would her reputation be at risk?"

"I heard an interesting piece of news this morning from a viewer who called in. It seems Shona and her father were overheard having a heated discussion in the Capitol Building. Voices were loud and tempers were hot, apparently. It also seems Kemper threatened to cut short her career. That sounds like something Shona would want to explain to the public if she had a chance. We can offer her that opportunity."

"Blackmail?"

Wendy leaned forward, offering Geoff a view of her décolletage, should he choose to indulge. He did not. "One way or another, we'll get Shona into this station and interview her. I don't think you want Megan interviewing her. She's got an eye for your spot at the news desk, and she looks really good on camera. Besides, she has a reputation for down-and-dirty interviews, and she's good at putting a spin on things."

"If you wanted to, you could make Shona look guilty to our viewers," Geoff said. "And you could even manipulate other personnel to do so. You've proven in the past that you're clever enough to make your insinuations in a way that you couldn't be sued for slander. But I don't think you'd risk the reputation of this station, because when Shona's name is cleared, then who will look bad? It'll look just like you're out for revenge."

Wendy shrugged. "I suppose if you're not interested, I'll give the interview to Megan." She left the dressing room.

Geoff's cell phone alerted him that he was receiving a text message. He seldom got those, though he had been sent several bible verses from Kemper in the past couple of weeks. The words came up on the screen, and Geoff felt a frisson of shock.

Daily devotional: Bible leaders
Moses the deliverer of Israel: Exodus 2:3 When she could no longer hide him she took for him an arc of bull rushes and daubed it with slime and with pitch and put the child therein…and the daughter of Pharoah came down to wash herself at the river…

The verses were broken, incomplete and intermingled. It was from Kemper. It made absolutely no sense at all.

TWELVE

Karah Lee's cell phone beeped just as she was making a second tour of the hotel's breakfast bar. She had always battled a weakness for breakfast, and it didn't help that one of her best friends in Hideaway, Bertie Meyer, owned a bed-and-breakfast with the most delicious breakfast bar in the four-state area.

Taylor's name and number came up on the tiny cell phone screen.

"Hey, Taylor, what's up?" she answered, eyeing a stack of waffles and bacon, alongside a vat of delicious smelling maple syrup.

"Morning." His voice was deep and rough.

She glanced at the tall grandfather clock in the far corner of the room. "It's nearly nine. Did you just get up?"

"I haven't even made it to bed yet."

"Why not?"

"I had pressing matters to attend to, such as finding someone to check out this computer for hackers."

"And?"

"Blaze and his teacher from the college have some results of their search. It seems Jerrod was looking for more than just your personnel files."

"He wouldn't have found more, because the clinic didn't have my medical files at the time."

"But he knew where to look because he saw the information on your personnel file, and knew where you lived and worked. Or at least he could make a pretty good guess."

"How about Dad's records and Shona's? Was there any evidence they were hacked into?"

"We don't have any way of knowing. We've made a few calls. Their files are being checked for any evidence of tampering."

"Will you let me know as soon as you find something?"

"Of course. Have you decided when the funeral is going to be?"

"Shona wants it done as quickly as possible, but there's an autopsy to be performed. I think the coroner's office will make it a top priority. If we can manage to have the service Monday, that would be best for all concerned."

"I'll be there," Taylor said.

"You don't have to do that."

"Yes, I do. This is your father. I love you, and he would have been my father-in-law. I'm going to be there for the funeral."

Karah Lee loved this man. "Thanks."

"I miss you."

She smiled. When they first met, it had not been apparent to her that Taylor Jackson was a romantic. He was big and gruff and tended to brood at times. But since they became engaged, his tender, soft side had emerged. He had become a man very much in love, and she a woman in love. She'd never thought it would happen to her.

The knowledge of his love chased away, for a few moments, the sorrow of this trip. She filled him in on the latest developments.

Too soon, however, Fawn sidled up with a pointed look at the bountiful plenty on Karah Lee's plate. Then, Taylor received another call and had to disconnect.

Later, there would be time for a quiet talk with him. Later never came often enough.

Shona shoved her cell phone into the front pocket of her jeans. Why Officer Marsh had dragged this solitary pair of denims from the back of the closet, she could not say.

Didn't the woman realize jeans were not Shona's style, unless she was attempting to raise money for a campaign by attending a rodeo or a hayride with a generous constituent? *Perhaps it's a joke on me.*

She slipped from the suite and walked to the end of the hallway, where she could look out over the parking lot. Sure enough, she saw a couple of reporters camped out in their cars near her Escalade. She would have to walk to the police station. It wasn't far.

She took the stairs instead of the elevator, craving a good, strong triple shot of espresso from the new Starbucks that Milt had mentioned. Decaf could wait for another day. This morning, she needed energy to get her started. Then on to the police station for fingerprinting.

Last night, she had retired early, leaving Geoff, Karah Lee and Fawn to visit in the living room while she called Jerrod with the news about Dad. He had seemed stunned and had ended the call quickly.

His reaction surprised her. He'd introduced himself to Karah Lee only a few months ago by showing her a photograph of himself as a child. He'd looked just like Shona. To her surprise and Karah Lee's, Dad had not insisted on any tests for proof, though Jerrod had offered to submit to them.

In fact, Dad had seemed excited about Jerrod's sudden appearance in his life.

Shona pulled her cell phone from her pocket and pressed her brother's speed dial number. He should probably give some input into Dad's funeral.

There was no answer. She left a message as she stepped into the hotel lobby. She was sliding the phone back into her pocket when she came face-to-face with a fortysomething man in jeans and a Kansas City Chiefs ball cap.

"Mrs. Tremaine? I'm Joe Baker with the *Kansas City Star.* I'm so sorry for your loss."

"Thank you." She moved to step past him, but he turned and walked beside her.

"I thought your father was a great man, and I would have voted for him for governor."

"I appreciate that. If you'll excuse me, I have a busy morning—"

"I've received a disturbing report from a reader this morning, and I'd like to give you a chance to refute it."

She slowed her steps, but didn't stop as she headed for the front doors. "What report would that be, Mr. Baker?"

"I was told a fight took place between you and your father a few days ago. Would you mind commenting on that?"

The impact of his words hit her harder than they had with the police. Word was out, and Dad was dead. Suddenly, grief struck her like a speeding train. She kept walking. "Yes, I'll comment on it." *Keep your voice steady, Shona.* "Had I known Dad was going to…to die last night, I would have moved heaven and earth to reconcile with him."

"What was the fight about?"

"It isn't important now."

"People are wondering if the fight could be connected to his death."

She cast him a level gaze. "I certainly hope you're not implying I would do something like that."

"Word has it that Senator MacDonald bled to

death, that a syringe was found in his chair at home. Do you think the killer might have been making a statement about the senator's last campaign slogan?"

Shona stumbled on the sidewalk.

"You know, the slogan?" he pressed. "Stop Bleeding Missouri Dry."

His words brought slicing pain and an anger so fierce she felt herself tremble with it. She clenched her hands at her sides and kept walking.

"Do you plan to run for your father's position?" the reporter asked, falling into step beside her.

She stopped and glared at him. "The plans I'm making today are for my father's funeral. Beyond that I have no idea what I'm going to do, and this morning I couldn't care less. I have no further comment for you. Now leave me alone!" She turned her back on him and raised her hand to a passing taxi.

As she sank into the backseat, her tears flowed freely. The nightmare was getting worse; no matter what she did, she couldn't escape it.

Geoff was still puzzling over his recent incoming message when he received another knock at his dressing room door barely ten minutes after Wendy's visit. He had a scowl on his face when he stepped out to find Detective Bradley Shane standing in the hallway.

"Bad day?" Shane asked.

"It hasn't been the best." Geoff held the door and gestured for the detective to come inside. "Have a seat. I take it you needed to talk with me about some-thing?" He perched on the dressing bench.

The detective nodded and settled into the recliner. "Where were you yesterday between the hours of noon and 7:30 p.m.?"

Uh-oh. This meant the focus was now on him, per-sonally, and not just for the information he could give them about Kemper's connections. "I was at the station from 10:00 a.m. until my director told me about the alleged shooting."

"You were here all the time? You never left the building?"

"That's right. I was then encouraged by my director to go to the hospital."

Shane opened his notebook. "Who first told you it was a shooting?"

"Wendy Phillips, my director. Originally, my wife told the dispatcher that she thought her father had been shot. Later, when I spoke with her, she simply said that Kemper said the word *shot* before he lost conscious-ness. We later learned there was no gunshot wound. I'm sure this was all covered last night with Shona."

"Yes, but we like to cover the facts over and over until we can get everything to line up."

"Of course."

"Did your wife tell you what else her father said before he lost consciousness?"

"Yes, he said to get away."

Shane's eyes narrowed. "What he said was, 'Get

away from Geoff.' We're trying to decide if the man meant Geoffrey Tremaine or Jefferson City."

Geoff kept his surprise to himself with great effort. That was what she couldn't tell him. But why not? Could she have thought he'd have tried to kill Kemper?

Another thought occurred to him, which he immediately tried to dismiss. And yet he couldn't. Shona was the only one who'd heard her father's final words. Was that what Kemper had really said?

Geoff became aware that the detective was watching him closely.

"Would the senator have had any reason to fear you, Mr. Tremaine?"

"Never."

"Can you think of anyone besides Mrs. Tremaine who had access to Senator MacDonald's mansion?" Shane asked.

"Other than myself, Shona and Kemper's household staff, I wouldn't know."

"What about the other daughter?"

"Karah Lee was in Hideaway, Missouri, when I called to tell her about Kemper. As you know, she's in Jefferson City now."

"I understand there was also bad blood between our senator and his younger daughter, Karah Lee."

"There were…unfortunate family dynamics. They fought a lot."

The detective glanced down at his notes. "My research shows Karah Lee MacDonald changed her name to Fletcher, her mother's maiden name, when her parents divorced. That reveals a lot of animosity."

"She was eighteen at the time, Detective Shane. I assure you that Karah Lee is a solid character. She isn't the kind of person who would slip into the mansion while her father is gone and set up syringes to kill him."

"Granted, it would take some planning and forethought to complete a setup like that." The man glanced down at his notes again. "Mr. Tremaine, do you have a key to the mansion?"

"Yes, I do."

"And do you know if members of Senator Mac-Donald's Drug Task Force would have access to the house?"

"No, I wouldn't."

"Is it likely? After all, the senator worked with Representatives Plinkett and Forester very closely over the past few months."

"But they were close friends. I would never suspect anyone on the task force of murder."

"They never had disagreements of any kind?"

"Of course, but—"

"Mr. Tremaine, a witness saw Senator MacDonald come to your house about two weeks ago one Friday evening. This morning, Detective Milt Davis told me you spoke with him late last night about the discussion you had with the senator. Would you mind telling me about that visit?"

Geoff was struggling to keep up with the detective's abrupt shifts in questioning. "He came to apologize for any part he might have played in the breakup of my marriage."

"Anything else?"

"He wanted me to attempt a reconciliation with my wife."

"That's all?"

Geoff hesitated. "My father-in-law was upset about an argument he'd had with Shona that day. I think something had been weighing on his mind for some time, and the argument underscored his self-doubts that he had been making a lot of wrong choices. He knew I was a Christian, and he wanted guidance. I don't know if you understand the Christian vernacular, but that night he repented for the way he had been living his life and asked God's forgiveness."

Shane gave Geoff a look of skepticism. "I hate to tell you how many times I've heard that."

"I've heard it before, too, though not from Kemper. This time, coming from him, I think it was sincere."

"Lots of people are sincere. It never changes things."

"Not if they're trying to change themselves. Kemper asked for help, and I believe he was getting it."

"From you?"

Geoff watched the man sadly. "From Christ. He had a change of heart. Life changing. I've been concerned that this change might have caused him to place himself in harm's way."

"What did he do?"

"Kemper took steps to make sure others knew he was sincere. He ended a relationship he felt was immoral. He also told me he was involved in a deal with the devil, and he was planning to break that deal."

The detective put his pen down and leaned forward. "So you're saying there was something about this…this spiritual change of his that might have made someone feel threatened? Perhaps enough to take the senator out?"

"It's possible, but he didn't tell me more." He thought about the text message he'd received from Kemper earlier. It had to be some kind of fluke, nothing more.

"No indication about whom this 'devil' might have been?"

"None. I do know he was seeking ways to raise money for his war chest for his campaign for governor. If he made some kind of deal with a wealthy individual who would pay him well for some political favors, he might have made someone quite angry when he went back on his word."

"He gave you no names, no descriptions, nothing?"

"Nothing."

The detective put his notebook away and stood. "Thank you for this information. If you happen to think of anything else, anything at all, you'll—"

"I'll be sure to call you."

Shane nodded and left.

THIRTEEN

Shona stared out the taxi window at the slowly passing buildings. Morning traffic was unusually heavy. Why hadn't she asked Karah Lee and Fawn to accompany her to the police station? Why did she have to be such a loner? Right now, she needed someone with her, and they had come here for just that reason. Why didn't she let them do what they had come here to do?

"Ma'am?"

The taxi driver was watching her impatiently. "This is the police station."

She realized where she was. She had asked the poor guy to drive her barely three blocks. "I've changed my mind. Take me to Starbucks." She would walk to the station from there…unless another lurking reporter decided to stalk her.

Oh, Dad, why? He was gone.

Why hadn't she taken steps to make amends? Yes, she'd been angry, but to give him the silent treatment for two weeks? How could she have behaved so childishly?

Now, she was grateful that she hadn't tendered her resignation, as she had intended to do. It would have made no difference in the end, except to burden her with even more grief and guilt. At least Dad had been spared that pain.

She was stepping from the taxi in front of Starbucks when her cell phone chimed. It was the TV station.

She answered quickly, eager to escape her thoughts. "Geoff?"

"Sorry. I should be so lucky to have him make this call," came a woman's deep voice.

"Wendy Phillips." As far as Shona could remember, the director of the Channel 6 television station had never called her before, though they had met a few times at social functions. Due to past conflicts, those meetings hadn't been exactly pleasant. "What can I do for you?"

"First of all, I'm sorry to hear about your father. I know this has to be hard for you." The woman's condolences sounded genuine. "Are you doing okay?"

Shona didn't trust what she was hearing. There had been too much animosity between Wendy and Dad.

"Thank you for your concern," Shona said dryly. "I'll be fine. What do you need?"

"It isn't what I need from you that counts right now, it's what your husband needs. If you care at all about his career, you could put as much effort into helping him keep his job as he is trying to protect your privacy. As I told him earlier, you are public property, in the public eye, and a story on you is fair game."

"Cut to the chase and tell me what you want," Shona snapped. "I'm busy."

"Geoff has placed his career in peril by refusing to allow you to be interviewed about your reactions to the senator's death."

Thank you, Geoff. Though he had gone to work for one of Dad's most outspoken detractors, he had always managed to keep Wendy from using him as a pawn to punish Dad.

In fact, Dad had wondered aloud more than once if Geoff hadn't actually used his influence to tone down the station's attacks on the MacDonald reputation.

"Does Geoff speak for you?" Wendy asked.

"I speak for myself, as I always have."

"Does this mean we might expect an interview in the future?"

"Why should I do that? You've done nothing but criticize my father—and therefore me—at every opportunity, and if you didn't have an opportunity you've created one."

"As of last night, everything has changed." Wendy really could sound sincere when she wanted to. "As I said, I'm sorry about your loss. A good interview would go a long way toward clearing your name in the public eye."

Wendy was bluffing; Geoff wouldn't lose his job.

The woman might be spiteful, but she wasn't stupid. Geoff was not only very charismatic at the news desk, he had been an excellent roving reporter before his promotion. He wasn't just a talking head.

"I don't need help to clear my name," Shona said. "The police will do that soon enough."

"You and I both know that if you're planning a future in politics, you will need more than just the police pulling for you," Wendy said. There was another pause. "You *are* planning a future in politics, aren't you?"

Shona didn't reply. She couldn't.

"Missouri memories are long," Wendy continued. "My father found that out the hard way. The sooner you make an effort to reassure the public of your innocence, the better your name will look on election day."

Suddenly appalled by that thought, Shona swallowed. "No matter what I plan for my future, I'm not so focused on a political agenda that I'm ready to use my father's death to publicize my own career."

"Then why don't you just focus on telling the public the truth? An interview would be the best way for you to reassure the people of Missouri that all the good your father did will not be undone."

Shona scowled. "Don't push it."

"I'm not. I'm giving you an opportunity."

Simply because this was Wendy Phillips, Shona considered hanging up on her. Unfortunately, the woman was right. Shona was human enough to want to clear her name in the public eye, whether she ran for office or not. She also needed to clear this scandal from the MacDonald name.

"Geoff may interview me this afternoon," Shona said. "If you can't prepare by that time, I might be willing to give you an evening slot, but no later. I have a funeral to plan and, believe it or not, that's my top priority right now."

"We can work it out. Are you sure you want Geoff to do it? Will you be able to do the interview without your personal relationship intruding?"

Shona wouldn't even attempt to explain her relationship with Geoff right now, because she didn't know what it was. "Are you questioning my professional integrity?"

Another brief pause. "Of course not."

"I'll only talk to Geoff, so take it or leave it. Keep Sally Newton out of my face or the deal is off. Now, if you'll excuse me, I have a few thousand things to deal with before our interview. Have a good day, Wendy." As Shona disconnected, she wondered again at Geoff's ability to work for the woman. However, at this point, she was glad he was well-positioned in the enemy camp. His presence there was proving highly protective.

Geoff received the expected call from Shona barely thirty minutes after his clash with Wendy. Neither of them had wasted much time. In the background, he heard the grind of an espresso machine.

"Getting your morning fix?" he asked.

"I needed to escape the hotel for a while." She sounded slightly hoarse, as if she hadn't had much sleep last night. "Your dragon called to schedule an interview."

"And?"

"She said you refused to allow me to be interviewed at the station."

"And you believed her?"

"I wouldn't believe anything that woman told me."

"Good."

"But I'm doing the interview."

"Okay, but—"

"I was very specific. I will talk to you and only you, and I will only be available this afternoon or evening."

"Today?" he exclaimed. "Shona, isn't that a little sudden?"

"Take it or leave it." There was an edge in her voice. "What did Dad want when he talked to you two weeks ago?"

Aha. That was the irritation. "We can discuss it soon."

"Oh, really? Have the police not asked you about it yet? Because they certainly asked me, and I didn't have any idea what the detective was talking about. Could it have any connection to Dad's murder?"

"I've already mentioned it to the police. I don't want to discuss it over the telephone."

"Dad never told me he talked to you," she said.

"I guess he didn't share everything with you."

There was an impatient sigh. "Do you want the interview or not?"

"Of course, I'll do it, but this is quite a turnaround from your attitude last night."

"Wendy was quick to point out that Dad was a public figure, as am I," Shona said. "Whether I like it or not right now. Wendy also implied it would save your job."

"Wendy makes big threats," Geoff said. "You do what you want, and don't allow Wendy or anyone else to manipulate you."

There was a long silence, and Geoff no longer heard the whirring in the background. Shona must have stepped outside. "Interview me, Geoff."

"Why the sudden push to do this? I know you are your father's daughter, but you've never sought the limelight for yourself."

"I need to clear my name. If the police can't do it, I at least want to address the issue and let people know I'm not trying to avoid it."

"It's a date. We'll tape at seven tonight."

"Fine. I'll talk to you then."

"I'll be looking forward to it."

FOURTEEN

On Saturday evening, Shona sat in a plush armchair adjacent to Geoff on the Channel 6 station set. As she had expected, he began gently, asking simple questions, trying not to trip her up or confront her in any way.

For that, she was grateful, because she felt battered. Several times, she'd had doubts about her impulsive offer to be interviewed so soon after her father's murder.

"Shona," he said, after breaking the ice with a few details of her experience the night before, "I know last night was a traumatic experience for you and that you can't answer specific questions, but do you have your own theories about what might have happened to your father?"

She responded carefully. "The autopsy revealed that he bled to death from the complications that resulted from an overdose of a blood thinner. As I've already stated, there is a murder investigation underway."

"Could this have been an accident? Did the senator take blood thinners for any reason?" Geoff asked.

"No. It is believed the substance was injected into him."

"Shona, I know this is painful, and you must be asking yourself why and how this could have happened. Have you come up with any answers?"

She nodded. "Earlier today someone remarked that the killer might have been trying to make a statement with this particular act, since my father won his latest election with the campaign slogan, Stop Bleeding Missouri Dry."

Geoff hesitated briefly. No one in the viewing audience was likely to pick up on it, but Shona did. He obviously hadn't thought about the implications.

"I know the senator favored some major budget cuts, but do you feel that could have been a motive for murder?"

"Who knows what would be a motive? I've never been inside the mind of a murderer."

"Shona, I know your loss is far too fresh for you to consider your options for the future…" He left the question hanging.

"That's right. My hope today is to simply plan a funeral that will honor my father's memory."

"However, it has been mentioned that your name is on the list of candidates for appointment to your father's position. If you are appointed would you fill that vacancy?"

Shona paused for only a few seconds before replying, but in that time she felt the impact of the question almost physically. What *was* she planning to do with her life?

Yesterday, as she prepared to submit her resignation, she had felt it would be necessary to give up a career in politics. Though she knew herself well enough to know she wouldn't be satisfied doing anything else, she also realized that her career—her whole life—hadn't been satisfying since her split with Geoff. Nothing had gone right without him.

She cleared her throat quietly, then spoke with slow deliberation. "As I've said, I would like to honor my father's memory. If I can best do that by filling the vacancy created by his passing, then that is what I'll do."

"You wouldn't want to take some time to back away from the whole situation and try to regroup?"

Yes, she definitely wanted time. She wanted the opportunity to find out what had gone wrong between them, and to repair the damage. "That's a luxury we can't afford," she said. "Not with the drug war in this state heating up, and one of the biggest opponents to illegal drug trafficking permanently out of commission."

"Do you feel your father's death could be connected to his tough stance against the drug traffic in this state?"

"I'm not prepared to make a further statement about the meaning of his death at this time," she said with a smile to soften the abruptness of her reply.

"We have an excellent police force, and they are hard at work searching for the killer."

"How likely do you feel it is that you'll be appointed in his place?"

Shona spread her hands. "The governor knows me, and he's familiar with my abilities. I know the job and projects on which Dad was working, as I worked closely with him on them. There are, however, many qualified individuals from whom the governor may choose. I'm sure he'll make the best choice."

"Shona, has last night's tragedy caused you to reconsider a life as a public servant?"

"No. If someone truly feels called to public service, then she shouldn't allow threats or rumor or danger to stop her from doing what she believes to be right." But love could certainly cause her to second-guess herself.

"Do you agree with your father's support of budget cuts?"

"I believe in having a balanced budget, yes."

"It's been apparent," Geoff continued, "that Senator MacDonald has been preparing you to run for office yourself. Do you think that's something you would consider in the near future?"

Shona met his gaze. Something about the tension in his voice told her the answer she gave might be important to him personally. "I didn't agree to this interview so I could campaign for office. I simply want to reassure the citizens of Missouri, and especially those faithful constituents who have supported my father, that his efforts to clean up Missouri's drug problem have not been in vain. The fight will continue, with or without me."

"Thank you." There was a heavy pause, and she knew the question he was preparing to ask. "Shona, there is a question that several callers have asked us today. You and your father were overheard arguing in his office two weeks prior to the senator's death. Can you tell us what that was about?"

"I can't tell you the particulars at this point, because even though both of us were talking loudly, it was a private discussion. If you're asking if I was angry enough with my father to commit premeditated murder, the idea is too preposterous to consider. I will forever regret that argument, and especially that my father and I never reconciled afterward."

She met and held Geoff's gaze for a brief moment, then he looked at the camera, smiled and said good-night.

As soon as the cameras were off, Geoff gathered the notes he had spread across the table and stood to leave. "Thank you for granting us this time, Shona. I still feel it wasn't necessary to do this when you're under so much—"

"Do you mind if we speak privately now?" she asked.

He hesitated as a sound technician reached for the tiny microphone attached to his lapel.

"Off the record?" she asked, removing her own sound piece and handing it to the tech.

"I wouldn't mind at all. Would you like to go somewhere for coffee? Decaf, of course."

No. Not out for coffee—it was too much like a date, too intimate. She wasn't ready for that. There were too many unanswered questions. "Why don't we just go to your dressing room?"

Had Geoff entertained any illusion that he had fallen out of love with his wife, he realized as he led the way to his dressing room that there was no such possibility. Every part of him was aware of her presence beside him. He was also painfully aware of the great chasm between them.

During all these months of separation, he had tried to pinpoint the exact time their marriage had encountered rocks. He'd attempted to analyze their history dispassionately, but discovered that was not possible. He could never be dispassionate about Shona.

He led the way into his dressing room, closing the door behind them.

She sank onto the bench in front of his dressing mirror, facing him. "Would you sit down for a moment? This won't take long."

He sat.

She clasped her hands in her lap, then looked down at them. "I've done a lot of thinking lately." She looked up at him then. "You know that's what I do best. I like to analyze things too much. Dad always complained about it."

"It's a good trait to have. I've been doing a lot of that myself lately."

"Have you drawn any conclusions?"

He held her gaze. "About what?"

She returned to the study of her hands. "Geoff, last night, before I found Dad, I was preparing to give him my resignation."

Geoff stared at her. His first inclination was to shout hallelujah. His second was to doubt her intentions. He didn't say anything. What could he say?

"I have known for several months that I made the wrong decision," she said.

He hated the sudden rush of suspicion that attacked him. How many times had her father done this same kind of thing, using the circumstances to his advantage, pretending that all was working out as it should when life threw him a curve?

Was she manipulating this situation the way her father had always done, pretending that she would have, at last, made the right choice?

And yet, why would he suddenly suspect that? She had never been like Kemper. Or, at least, not during the early years of their marriage, before she started turning a blind eye to her father's maneuverings.

She leaned forward. "I should not have left you. I should have stayed and tried to work things out. Working for Dad was becoming more and more onerous these past months, and I disagreed with him often, though not as vocally as I did two weeks ago."

He wanted to tell her that he had known as soon as she made the choice that it was wrong. He'd told her at the time that she was wrong.

"Tell me what you're thinking, Geoff."

"I don't think I should," he said quietly.

"When you gave Dad your resignation last year you gave me a choice. You said I could quit when you did, or I could stay with my father. You made me choose between you and my father—not just my father, but my whole career."

"That isn't fair. Your career was never limited to Kemper. I tried to warn you—"

"I know. He was a part of the good-old-boys club, and he called in favors to benefit himself, bowed to special interests and allowed his vote to be bought instead of holding out for the welfare of his constituents, regardless of popularity. I didn't need a list of my father's sins, Geoff. I didn't then and I don't now. I knew what he was. I also believed, at the time you quit, that he still believed he was doing the right thing most of the time for the state."

"Maybe he did believe that, but did you?"

"I'm telling you, last night I was planning to resign."

Geoff still couldn't tell her what he thought. Her father had just been murdered. She was wounded and fragile. She didn't need him heaping more guilt on her.

There was a passage in the Bible that warned Christians to be as wise as serpents and as harmless as doves. Kemper had actually taught Geoff, by example, that it was always best to be suspicious of the motives of others.

"I'm sorry, Shona. Perhaps we should talk about this some other time."

She raised a hand to her face and rubbed her brow wearily. "I suppose I should have expected this."

He noticed her hand was trembling slightly. Was that an act, an attempt to win his sympathy?

Where was all this bitterness coming from? He thought he'd forgiven her.

"You don't believe me, do you?" she asked.

"I'm sorry, Shona. I'd love to."

"I've never been a liar."

That was one of the things he had once admired about her. "Too much has happened. Or perhaps, I should say too much hasn't happened in the past eleven months. You've never given any indication that you'd had a change of heart."

She leaned forward, her eyes pleading with him to listen. "You're wondering why I didn't tell you this sooner?"

He nodded. "I'm also wondering why you didn't tell me what Kemper said to you last night."

"I told you—"

"You didn't tell me everything. You didn't tell me what you told the police, about your father warning you to get away from me. Or was that Jeff City he was talking about?"

She looked down at her hands, which were clasped tightly in her lap. "The time never seemed right."

"Is that it? Or did you harbor some doubts about me last night? As I said, we should save this conversation for later. You've had a horrible time. Your world has been turned upside down. Give it some space." Did she truly expect him to believe she had been ready, just last night, to return to the marriage on which she had turned her back last year? And yet, just tonight she had publicly expressed her willingness to step into her father's position, even to run for office if the time was right.

"I'm sorry," she said. "I suppose I shouldn't have expected you to welcome me with open arms. After all, we did have a lot of issues."

"I'm not worried about those issues. We could always have worked those out."

"But we didn't before, did we? All we did was fight."

He gave her a searching look, then sadly shook his head. "Shona, if you had come to me before Kemper's death, I would have been overjoyed." He spread his hands. He didn't feel that was what was happening here. He felt manipulated.

"How could you have known me all these years and still be able to believe I'm that kind of a game player?"

"I never said you were a game—"

"I've never tried to deceive you or be something I

was not." She stepped toward the door. "You know what? I believed you knew me better than that, but apparently more has been destroyed in our marriage than I'd thought. Maybe we really can't work things out."

She pulled the door open.

Geoff was preparing to stop her when Wendy came careening through the doorway. "Well, it looks as if our show has brought out the crazies tonight."

"Why is that?" Geoff demanded, irritated by the interruption, irritated by Shona, but mostly irritated by his own response to Shona, because he no longer felt capable of trusting the one woman whose word he had always believed. And she obviously no longer felt capable of trusting him.

"We've had our first crank call of the weekend," Wendy said. "Guy says he thinks somebody had better be watching Shona's back, because if she's planning to campaign for her father's position, she'll end up just like her father. He said if someone else doesn't do it, he'll do it himself."

"That's silly," Shona said. "No one's going to try to poison me."

Geoff's irritation increased. "How do you know that? Do you suddenly think you're exempt from attack?"

"No, I think this supposed 'crank call' is a fabulous way to jump in the ratings, just as tonight's interview was."

"How can you say that after your own father

warned you to get away from this city?" Geoff demanded. "I suggest you listen to him."

Shona gave Geoff another glare, then turned and stalked from the studio.

"Hmph," Wendy said. "I guess that interview went well."

FIFTEEN

Karah Lee had read the first page in her new novel for the third time when the suite door opened and Shona stepped inside. She looked drained. Her face was pale, her eyes smudged with shadows.

"Great interview, but are you crazy?" Karah Lee said softly.

Shona scowled at her. "Don't you start, too. Where's Fawn?"

Karah Lee pointed toward the closed bedroom door. "She wanted to watch TV and I wasn't in the mood. Shona, you have a chance to take a break from politics for a while, and here you're practically announcing your candidacy for state senator."

Shona slumped onto the sofa, then looked up when the bedroom door opened and Fawn came out.

"Hi, Aunt Shona. You looked great on television." She swooped in for a hug. "Don't let Karah Lee give you a hard time. I'm proud of you."

Some of the heaviness lifted from Shona's expression. "Thanks. I need to keep you around. What do you say to a long visit with your old auntie this summer?"

"Or you could come and stay with us for a month or two. Don't politicians get some downtime?"

Shona glanced at Karah Lee and nodded. "It could happen."

"Wonders never cease," Karah Lee drawled. "We might see if you could sublet an apartment from Grace Brennan. She seldom uses her apartment above her mom's shop now that she's got a hit single out and is traveling all over the country."

Fawn gave Shona a kiss and returned to her show in the other room, and the light in Shona's eyes dimmed once more. "That kid doesn't know the meaning of the word shy."

"She likes people, and people immediately like her."

"Maybe she would do well in politics."

"Don't even think about it," Karah Lee said. "And don't suggest that to her. I think she'd make a great doctor. I've thought about enrolling her in pre-med. It would be heartbreaking to lose her to a larger university in Columbia or Kansas City, but—"

"Make it Columbia. She can live with me and commute."

Karah Lee studied her sister's expression. "And where will you be living?"

Shona frowned. "I haven't decided. Why do you ask?"

"Just curious. As I said, your interview with Geoff

was good. You were actually civil to him, made eye contact, the whole bit. I could tell he wasn't happy with your apparent willingness to jump right back into the ring, though."

"That's too bad."

"So what happened after the interview?"

"What do you mean?"

"Something's really brought you down."

Shona looked at her quizzically, and for a very brief moment Karah Lee felt transported in time to their teen years, when Shona and Geoff were dating, and Shona would come home and tell her all about it before they went to bed. Just for that moment, they were sisters and best friends again.

Shona leaned her head against the back of the sofa and closed her eyes. "Last night, after the dinner, I was going to give Dad my resignation." The eyes squeezed more tightly shut, and twin droplets spilled down her cheeks. "Geoff didn't believe me when I told him after the interview."

"Oh."

Shona's head came up. "You believe me, don't you?"

Karah Lee made a face. "Well…"

"Don't you?"

"You would never turn your back on your political career, and you had just expressed your willingness to continue in Dad's place to a whole viewing audience."

"That's because everything's changed since yesterday. Dad is gone, and I truly believe what I said. Now is not the time to give up and allow the illegal drug manufacturers to ride roughshod over Missouri."

"But you tried to convince Geoff you were willing to leave Dad to fight the druggies alone as recently as last night? Come on, Shona. What do you expect him to believe?"

Geoff sat in a quiet booth in a far corner of The Rib and watched the entrance. The restaurant was usually packed with a boisterous crowd, and Saturday nights were the busiest, but by the time he'd arrived, the crowd had dispersed.

He couldn't help wondering about Shona. He hadn't been able to stop thinking about her words tonight—and her possible duplicity. What was he supposed to think when she couldn't bring herself to tell him what Kemper had said?

His cell phone gave a text messaging alert, and Geoff tensed, remembering the cryptic message this morning. He hit Receive, and the mystery deepened.

Important message KJV
Daily devotional: Bible leaders Matthew 16:17
Blessed art thou, Simon Bar-jona; for flesh and blood hath not revealed it unto thee, but my Father, who is in heaven…

For a moment, Geoff couldn't breathe. His middle name was Simon. What was happening here? Were these riddles of some kind? And why?

"Oh, Lord," he whispered, "what's happening here?" He felt as if he were getting a message from the dead, and yet he knew better. If Kemper was behind this, he would have set it up before his death. "Father, if there's something that does need revealing, I'm available."

The front door opened and Linda Plinkett stepped inside, on time as always, with a bemused half smile on her face. She eased into the booth across from Geoff and gave an exasperated shake of her head. "Really, Geoff, barbeque?"

He slipped the cell phone into his pocket and tried to focus on the conversation at hand. It was hard. "I've had a craving."

Her smile widened, and she leaned forward. "Barbeque isn't what you need, sweetheart. You need your wife back."

"Do you have reason to believe that's going to happen?"

She shrugged. "Just intuition. It was obvious to me, watching the interview tonight, that you two are still crazy about one another, though you're both too stubborn to admit it. Why are you here with me instead of trying to work things out with her?"

"I haven't had a good plate of ribs in months. They're Shona's favorite food in the world."

She chuckled. "Sounds as if I'm going to be hearing about Shona all night. I can see right now you're the kind of guy who would ask a lady out to dinner, then talk about another woman throughout the meal."

He smiled at her. *This* beautiful woman was the epitome of charm. Her deep-set brown eyes were so dark they appeared black, the contoured, feminine features of her face belying the herculean strength of her personality. Her hair, shoulder-length and loosely falling over her shoulders, was nearly as dark as her eyes. She had long ago perfected what Kemper Mac-Donald once referred to as the "come hither" look. She had a sharp mind and tough negotiating skills, but her edge, particularly with certain susceptible men, was in her appearance.

He did not count himself among those hapless men. "I promise to try not to talk about Shona," he said. "But since you brought the subject up, I heard that, once upon a time, you were on the verge of becoming her stepmother."

Linda's expression of cool amusement died. "Did she tell you that?"

"She won't tell me anything. Kemper and I had a good talk not long ago, though."

He could almost see her mind working behind the expression of carefully controlled disinterest. Her eyes narrowed. "Funny the things you can hear. *I* heard through the grapevine that you were on the police's list of suspects. Are you playing detective in order to work your way off the list?"

"We have law enforcement personnel crawling all over the city. They don't need me in their way."

She leaned forward and asked softly, "Do you suspect me?"

"Why can't I be curious about my father-in-law's personal relationships without suspecting someone of murder?"

"Because you're Geoff Tremaine and you have a reporter's instincts." She leaned forward. "Don't try to bluff me, my dear. You asked me here to interrogate me." She gave the dining area a look of distaste. "But if you were going to grill me, couldn't you at least have made sure the setting was more refined?"

"You don't like the mural of the mule in the lounge?"

She smiled. "Oh, it has a certain charm." She indicated her silk blouse. "I'm afraid I'll have to forego the heavy sauce, though. I don't have clothes that can withstand it."

"Mind if I ask you a few questions?"

"You can ask me all the questions you want to ask, but I have a few things I want to say to you, and you will listen." She sat back with a smile. "Relax. This will be fun."

Shona sipped at the chamomile tea Karah Lee handed her, then stared out at the lights of the city. "In the past few weeks I've realized I could no longer do things Dad's way. I was losing too much of my integrity when I turned a blind eye to some of his deals."

"Such as?"

"There's a limit to how much he could receive from each constituent for campaign funds, but he set up the finances so he could funnel excess contributions into renamed, separate accounts that he could switch over when funds were needed."

"Who was giving him the extra money?"

"I'm not sure. Dad kept records in his head to which I was never privy. He sold special favors."

"What if he didn't follow through on his part of any of those?" Karah Lee asked. "That might have been dangerous, if he reneged on the wrong constituent."

Shona nodded absently.

"What else happened tonight?"

"What makes you think anything did?"

"You're still distracted. You'd never make a good poker player. Are you still mad because Geoff wouldn't believe your story?"

"It wasn't a story, it was the truth."

"What else happened?"

Shona rolled her eyes. "Wendy Phillips came rushing to Geoff's dressing room after the show, reporting that the station had received a threatening phone call from a viewer. I wouldn't put it past her to make up something like that."

"It could have been the truth," Karah Lee said.

"How that woman manages to run a respectable television station is beyond me, but think of the ratings a death threat will generate."

"You don't think it's possible you really could be in danger?" Karah Lee asked. "Dad was controversial, and someone did kill him. If that same someone thinks you're going to follow in his footsteps—"

"It was nothing, okay? If anyone did actually call—which I doubt—it was probably some lonely person needing attention and this was the best, fastest way to get it."

Karah Lee decided not to argue. Shona was on a sharp edge right now.

Earlier that afternoon Shona and Karah Lee had selected a casket and planned most of their father's funeral service. Tomorrow, Karah Lee and Fawn would make a few final decisions about the service, while Shona focused on the eulogy.

Shona had also spent some time during the day devising an emergency plan of action should she be appointed by the governor to complete her father's term in office. Karah Lee fully expected that to happen.

Selfishly, however, and for the sake of her sister, she didn't want it to.

"I wonder how Geoff's dinner with Linda is going tonight," she said.

Shona looked at her. "Tonight? He's having dinner with her this soon?"

"Sure. I called him before the interview to warn him to take it easy on you and to find out all he could from Linda about Dad's interpersonal communications the past few months. He told me he was meeting her at The Rib this evening."

Shona nodded, frowning. Then a smile suddenly softened her face. "Remember when Geoff was dating Tess Younker, our junior year in high school?"

"Oh, you mean the night you dragged me out of bed to spy on them at the dance? Don't tell me you're bringing that up now because you're thinking about doing it again."

Shona's smile died swiftly. "Probably wouldn't be a good idea. We're not kids anymore. This is a murder investigation."

"Do you think Geoff will get any significant information from Linda?"

"I don't know. Maybe. But I keep thinking about the Beaufont Corporation."

"Organized crime," Karah Lee said. "And don't forget who Dad accused of having connections with organized crime."

"Randall Phillips, but Dad was never able to prove it."

"That doesn't mean it was a lie. One of the reasons I never told him what was going on in my life was because he seemed to have a finger in every pie in the state, and he was always trying to make things easier for me, which in the end just made things harder. He could have gotten that information about Phillips from a confidential source, but couldn't resist using it."

"Well, if Dad had a finger in every pie in Missouri, Beaufont has a finger in every illegal pie in Missouri. It just makes sense that they've clashed from time to time."

"I only remember the time I caused the clash," Karah Lee said. Last year she had called Dad for protection against the Beaufont Corporation when they sent a hit man after Fawn.

"He was so tickled his younger daughter finally asked him for something, he'd have done anything," Shona said.

"But I was the one who caused that confrontation and I'm the one who encouraged Dad to meet with Jerrod."

"What's that got to do with anything?"

Karah Lee stared out the window at the lights beyond. "I've discovered that not only was Jerrod hacking into my personnel files a few months ago, he also found a way into my medical files, as well as into yours and Dad's."

Shona grew still. She turned and met Karah Lee's gaze. "Our medical files?"

"Beaufont and Jerrod are both suspects. Is it possible that I was instrumental in leading Dad's killer to him?"

SIXTEEN

Linda ordered a rib salad and water with lemon. Geoff ordered a rack of ribs and root beer. As soon as the waiter left, Linda leaned forward once more.

"I don't suppose you would want to share what Kemper told you about our…friendship."

Geoff wasn't startled by her straightforward question, and he knew she would want an equally straight answer. They had known each other long enough and well enough that he could be frank with her. "Kemper told me only that he regretted his infidelities in the past and that he was going to do all he could to rectify the situation."

Linda's expression clouded. "That's what he called our friendship, an infidelity?"

"He always had the utmost respect for you, but I don't think he felt that the relationship you shared in the past few months showed that respect. Kemper finally decided, after all these years, that he actually did believe some of those sermons he'd heard when he was campaigning for votes on the church route. He also felt your relationship was setting the wrong example for your daughter."

She sat back in her seat with a sigh of resignation. "He tried to tell me something about that, but at the time I wasn't exactly in the mood to hear it. Kristin even mentioned it to me once. Kemper told me about the fight he had with Shona."

"It was too public. The media was bound to catch wind of it."

"I'm glad you gave her a chance to address the issue. I only hope the police will realize they've got the wrong person on their suspect list."

"I heard again today that the FBI is taking an interest in the case," Geoff said. "So far, the local police are the only authorities questioning me."

The waiter brought their drinks, and Linda thanked him, then leaned forward again. "The police are making a mistake if they don't do a little more research into Kemper's son's past."

"Karah Lee's fiancé, Taylor Jackson, did a background search soon after Jerrod introduced himself. He's legit."

"I still think there's something…off center about Jerrod's relationship to Kemper."

"Why is that?"

Linda trailed a finger down the water beads of her glass. "Kemper spent a lot of time with his son these past few months, though I don't think he ever talked to Shona about it."

"Why not?"

Linda shook her head. "You would have to ask Jerrod that. I know Kemper was fascinated by Jerrod's ability to do computer hacking."

"Yet Kemper told you and not Shona?"

"He's always confided in me more than he has anyone else. Even when he and Irene were still speaking to each other, that didn't stop him from sharing his heart with me. There weren't a lot of people he could trust."

"What did he and Jerrod do? Just hang out? Jerrod lives in Olathe, Kansas, doesn't he? That's a couple of hours from here."

"There were a lot of times I know Shona thought Kemper was at my house when he was actually taking in a ball game with Jerrod. Those two bonded quickly."

"Why does that seem suspicious to you?"

"Call me a cynic, but in all the years Jerrod could have contacted his father, he didn't. Then suddenly, only months before his father is murdered, Jerrod is suddenly bosom buddies with him?" She shook her head. "Something doesn't ring true."

"Did you ever meet Jerrod?"

"Of course. Kemper was proud of him, and so thrilled to have found him. I think he was close to introducing Jerrod to the media as his son. That kind of authenticity is very attractive. A dangerous thing to have in this business, but attractive, nonetheless."

"Authenticity is never a bad thing to have."

She shrugged. "Not if it's you or Shona. You two are idealistic to a fault. Quite frankly, I'm surprised Shona lasted with Kemper as long as she did. I was almost sure she would resign when you did. I can tell you, Kemper was sweating it. I think he received many of his votes in the last election because he kept you and Shona in the public eye throughout the campaign. When things fell apart with you last year, that was when he began to lose hope for the campaign for governor. He did some pretty fast talking to get Shona to stay with him."

"I wish she hadn't."

"For her sake and yours, so do I, but I've never been one to brood on 'if onlys.' What's going to happen between you and Shona now? Think you can make amends?"

"I don't know if that's possible now, Linda. Somewhere along the line, we seem to have forgotten how to trust one another."

"Well, learn again before it's too late. You've got a marriage hanging in the balance, and it's uncertain whether or not Shona will be appointed to Kemper's position. She's done a great job, and she's the one who worked most closely with him. She was the one who kept him honest many times."

"I thought Paul Forester had undertaken that responsibility years ago."

Linda's expression suddenly cooled. "Paul likes to be in control or he throws a tantrum, and he likes to call the shots. Shona's tantrums are gentler and more effective."

"Everyone knows that."

"Paul read the riot act to Kemper and me more than once in the past months, and his propensity for running the show can be quite annoying. He was on the drug task force before Kemper and I joined him." Linda leaned forward and lowered her voice. "Things can get ugly here in the city. You don't want Shona in politics, do you?"

"What I want doesn't matter."

"You might be surprised what matters to Shona. In fact, *she* might even be surprised. She cares a great deal about what you think. I've seen that in the months since you've been separated. Every time your name comes up, she gets melancholy. Kemper told me many times that she never missed the evening news."

He thought about his argument with Shona at the station. Had she really been planning to give Kemper notice?

"Shona and Karah Lee will inherit a fortune. Neither of them will ever have to work again if they don't want to. I know Karah Lee's a dedicated doctor, but I can see Shona retiring from politics and investing her time in humanitarian efforts across the state. She could have more of an impact on those people for whom she has the most concern—the elderly, poor and children—if she isn't up to her neck in political maneuverings. And maybe she would have time for the two of you to make your marriage work."

"I thought you said you needed her on the drug task force."

"She could still assist us from the sidelines. You can't imagine the effort it's taken to compile and interpret data about the state meth activity. Shona was the one who pointed out that Missouri's reputation for drug activity is actually unfair. We've made a record number of meth-lab busts in this state because of the fantastic efforts of our law enforcement. We're going to keep up the fight. I know Shona believes in it, but she doesn't have to be a key player to help it work."

"Do you think Kemper's tough stance on the drug problem might have been what got him killed?"

Linda leaned back and stared at her glass for a moment, a sheen of tears in her eyes. "I honestly don't know, Geoff. I hope not. I know he took a much harder line on it than Paul ever did, but Kemper got more things done." She looked up at him, spreading her hands. "If I had any idea about who might have done it, I'd have told the police when they questioned me. I wish I could help you, but I'm at a loss."

* * *

Karah Lee finally reached her brother on the telephone after Shona and Fawn had gone to bed. Jerrod's voice was as deep as she remembered. As always, there was a hesitance in his speech, a note of caution, as if he was holding something back or was a bit suspicious.

"You're a hard man to reach," she said by way of greeting. "We tried to call you earlier today to ask if you'd like any input into the funeral."

"I got Shona's message. Thanks for asking. I don't know much about planning a funeral."

"I know this must be hard for you, especially since you lost your mother last year."

"Thanks."

"Jerrod, this is very awkward, but something has turned up during the investigation, and it's possible you could be questioned about it."

He waited.

"When we first met, you had hacked into my personnel files. You explained that you wanted to make sure I was really your sister before you introduced yourself to me."

"That's right."

She hesitated. There was no delicate way to ask her next question. "Did you need to know something about my medical history, as well? And Dad's and Shona's?"

She heard a swift intake of breath, and then a heavy sigh. "I...I'm sorry, Karah Lee. I've been so accustomed to having any information I need at my fingertips that when I needed to know something about family health history, I chose to find it myself instead of asking. I know that was wrong, but…well, I guess it's just easier to hide behind a computer than pick up the phone and call a stranger and…and bare my soul."

"Did you get the information you needed?"

"Yes. I spoke to Dad about it."

"You know, I *am* a doctor. You could have asked me."

Silence.

"You don't want to talk about it?"

"I will. I'll have to. It isn't something I want to talk about over the telephone. Has a definite time been set for the funeral?"

"Yes. The autopsy was given priority and they completed it today. The funeral will be Monday morning. Will you be attending?"

"Yes. Of course. I…I just wish I'd had more time to get to know Dad."

"I know exactly how you feel," she said softly. "I'll see you Monday."

Geoff was driving away from the restaurant when he made a telephone call—which he hoped would be his final conversation of the evening.

Paul Forester had been like an uncle to Shona and Karah Lee when they were growing up. A blustery old curmudgeon who prided himself on his reputation for honesty, Paul had been instrumental in urging Kemper to jump into politics in the first place. He was a much-respected icon in the state legislature.

Geoff knew Paul seldom went to bed before midnight, and was often at his best late in the evening.

"Geoffrey Tremaine," Paul greeted him. "Great to hear from you."

"Hi, Paul. You probably saw my interview with Shona tonight." Paul never missed the news. He often said it was his direct line to the lifeblood of the people of Missouri.

"It wasn't the smartest thing she's done," Paul said softly. "Exposing herself like that when Kemper's killer could still be on the prowl. Couldn't you have stopped her?"

"I tried. She threatened to contact another television station if I didn't interview her. I figured I could do damage control."

Paul chuckled. "That's our Shona. Never let anyone set her parameters for her."

"She wants the public to know she's innocent."

"Who would doubt that?"

"The police. The FBI. The public who heard about her fight with Kemper."

"Crazy. Is she planning to run for Kemper's office, if she isn't appointed?"

"I'm not sure. I hope she decides to take a breather."

Paul grunted. "She's her father's daughter. Her

act's a lot cleaner, and she's quite a bit prettier. This must be very hard for her."

"Yes, it is, but she's handling it well, for the most part."

"I'm glad you're supporting her. Tell me, Geoff, have the police checked out that housekeeper of Kemper's? I'd look at her closely if I were investigating the case. She's the one who lost the most with the budget cuts Kemper pushed for. I hear her husband lost his financial assistance when that epilepsy drug fell by the wayside."

"I've heard the same."

"I've also heard some other interesting information, which I gave the police today. Seems Mrs. Reynolds's nephew, who was living with her and her husband, was caught with drugs and paraphernalia about a month ago. The laws we've put into place are a lot stricter now. Mrs. Reynolds might just have several reasons for suddenly disliking Kemper."

"You really think she's a possible killer?"

"Never can tell. It's always those quiet ones we have to worry about. What are Shona's plans after the funeral?" Paul asked. "I was hoping she would get out of town, go stay with Karah Lee for a week or two."

"I doubt there's a chance of that. And I doubt there's a chance Shona would fire the housekeeper."

"That's what Karah Lee told me. Shona isn't budging. I have to tell you, I'm worried about that young lady."

"So am I, but what can I do? She isn't listening to me right now."

There was a heavy grunt. "You might be surprised, my friend. Shona has never recovered from your separation. If I were you, I'd see what I could do to repair things."

"You sound like Linda Plinkett."

"I could do without the insults, please."

"Sorry. Aren't you two getting along right now?"

"We do when we have to." There was a pause. "I didn't approve of her little tryst with Kemper. That kind of affair gives every politician a black eye."

"I guess you probably knew that Kemper and Linda had ended that recently."

"Yes. I don't see how it could have gone on, considering that business with Linda's daughter a few months ago."

Geoff stopped for a traffic signal. "Kristin? I thought she'd been living with her father since the divorce two years ago."

"She's in and out with both her parents. Poor kid became pregnant when she was here. She told Linda that Kemper was the father."

A car honked, and Geoff looked up to find the light was green. Shocked at Paul's revelation, he stomped the accelerator and shot across the intersection.

"You still there?" Paul asked.

"I'm here. Do you have any idea if the police have this information?"

There was a bark of unamused laughter. "You think it's a motive for murder?"

"It's a possibility."

"Well, if my teenage daughter turned up pregnant by an old codger like Kemper, I might resort to manslaughter. But Linda has more class than I do. She could easily have ruined Kemper's career in this state by telling the public about what he did."

"Not if she wanted to protect her daughter."

After saying goodbye to Paul, Geoff realized he still needed to have one more conversation that night—with Detective Bradley Shane.

SEVENTEEN

Rain hovered in the clouds above the steeple of the First Baptist Church of Jefferson City at nine-thirty, the morning of the funeral. Karah Lee and Fawn entered the vestibule of the church with Shona. The chapel was already filling with people. It was thirty minutes before the service was scheduled to begin. They would have a packed house.

"I still don't know why you wanted to use this church," Shona muttered to Karah Lee under her breath. "Dad never attended here."

Karah Lee was getting tired of her sister's foul mood. "He never attended anywhere regularly."

"Don't start."

"This is a beautiful building, one of the largest churches in town. Besides, Geoff attends here."

Shona gave Karah Lee a look of surprise. "He does?"

"Yes, so he was able to request permission to use it."

"You really have kept in touch with him, haven't you?"

"He's still my brother-in-law." Karah Lee glanced toward Fawn, who looked sophisticated in a navy suit, her short blond hair combed starkly away from her face in a style only someone with her gamine features could pull off successfully.

Fawn left the side of an elderly lady and returned to Karah Lee.

Shona excused herself quietly and stepped to the balcony stairway, which had been cordoned off.

Fawn nudged Karah Lee and pointed toward the entrance, where Kemper's long unknown son, Jerrod Houston, entered. Now that Karah Lee knew him better, she could easily see his resemblance to Shona, in the black hair, the dramatically arched eyebrows, and the dark gray eyes.

He had their father's physique, though he didn't carry himself with as much authority as Kemper had. Jerrod walked as if a heavy weight rested on his shoulders, and he often kept his gaze downcast to the floor.

He spotted Karah Lee and Fawn and started toward them.

"He looks so good he makes my eyes hurt," Fawn murmured under her breath.

"Don't embarrass him," Karah Lee warned as she stepped forward to greet her brother. "You'll sit with the family during the service, won't you?" she asked him.

He glanced anxiously at the crowd, shaking his head.

"Sure you will, Uncle Jerrod," Fawn said, taking his arm. "Nobody'll think anything about it. They'll just figure you're a cousin or something."

He was obviously still reluctant to consider himself a part of the family. He hadn't taken part in the funeral arrangements, and he'd been adamant that his name shouldn't be mentioned in the obituary.

"I think Dad would have wanted you to be counted as part of the family," Karah Lee assured him.

"It'll make people curious."

"We're here to honor the memory of our father today, not worry about the curiosity of the public."

Karah Lee caught sight of her stepmother, Irene, entering on the arm of a tall, attractive man, and wondered at the woman's audacity. Granted, Dad and Irene had been separated, but—

Someone touched her arm. "Karah Lee?" It was Geoff.

"Hey. I wondered when you'd get here."

"Did Shona come with you?"

"We rode with her." Karah Lee nodded toward the staircase. "She's up there."

"I saw Taylor out in the parking lot. He's on his way in."

Karah Lee glanced toward the door. She had been afraid he would be stuck in Hideaway, busy as he was with calls.

"He'll be here soon." Geoff nodded to Jerrod, winked at Fawn, and followed in Shona's wake.

Karah Lee shivered, glancing at the steady line of people walking through the foyer. She knew what Shona was doing in the balcony. She was studying the faces of all those people she had thought she'd known so well. She was looking for the face of a killer. She wouldn't admit it, but that was what she was doing.

Was there a killer in the crowd looking for *her?*

Shona stood in the loft above the chapel as mourners filled the pews below. She recognized Randy Staponski, son of the late, great Earle Staponski, representative from Pierce City. Linda Plinkett, always meticulous, always attractive, wore a close-fitting black suit. She moved with smooth grace behind the usher toward the reserved section.

Shona had always admired Linda's poise and grace under fire, her sharp mind and her ability to rally people of varying political loyalties behind a common cause.

"I thought I'd find you up here," came Geoff's voice from behind her.

She turned to find him coming toward her from the head of the stairs, his blue gaze steady, his steps halting, as if a cautious approach might prevent another fight from breaking out between them.

Once again, she regretted blurting everything to him Saturday night. Why was it she could handle affairs of the state with calmness and tact, but when it came to her personal relationships she suddenly lost all discretion and social skills?

"Strategic position," he said, "always studying the seating arrangements, predicting allegiances."

"Could you manage to stifle the disapproval for today, at least?"

"Who said I disapproved?" He came to stand beside her and gaze down at the crowd. "I do feel you would be wise to remain on your guard in light of Saturday night's call."

"No one's going to try to kill me in this place. I still think it was simply a crank call, if anything."

"So you're looking for Kemper's killer. Do you really think he—or she—will show up here?"

"Maybe. To gloat. Isn't that what killers do?" She heard the bitterness in her own voice. "Indulge in the suffering of others?" She watched the funeral director seat three elderly ladies who had always worked for Dad on his campaigns. Shona had always loved Phyllis, Ethel and Vera.

"Have you heard from the governor?" Geoff asked

"Not yet."

Geoff was silent for a moment, then he said, "Even if the governor doesn't appoint you, do you plan to run in the next election?"

"I don't know for sure what I'm going to do. Right now I'm consumed with the overwhelming responsibility of tidying things up for whoever does take Dad's place."

"And you're looking for a killer."

"Whoever did this can't be allowed to get away with it, Geoff. Why did you come up here?" she asked. "I doubt it was just to play bodyguard."

With a sigh, he gazed out over the crowd. "I'm sorry. I didn't come here to argue with you again. I thought it might be a good time to tell you about your father's visit to me two weeks ago. Maybe it'll put your mind at ease."

She looked up at him. "You said he wanted to help you and me reconcile."

"That wasn't the only thing he wanted. I didn't tell you everything because he asked me not to. He wanted to tell you himself, in his own time, because he didn't think you were ready to believe him. I think it could bring you comfort now."

"What wouldn't I believe?"

"He was sorry for a lot of things he had done, and he was making some drastic changes in the way he lived his life."

"That's all? Dad made those kinds of promises before." She caught herself. "Oh, would you listen to me? Now I sound like my sister."

"He was sincere this time, Shona. He turned his life over to the only One who could really help him change."

Shona closed her eyes. If only she could believe that. Why had it become so hard for her to trust?

Because she'd heard her father's promises of change too many times and had been disappointed.

"I think he saw too much about himself that he didn't like," Geoff said. "And I think your argument with him that day in the office might have helped him see that need for change."

"So you're saying I jump-started his conscience?" she asked.

"I'm saying it's possible. He told me he knew he was the reason for our separation and he was willing to do whatever it took for us to reconcile. He even offered to evict you from the mansion." Geoff paused. "He thought about firing you."

"That's ridiculous. He wouldn't do that."

Geoff smiled. "I think he was emphasizing his willingness to do whatever it might take for us to reunite."

"How sad that it's come to this, then." She saw another familiar figure below—Uncle Paul. "What did you tell him?"

"That I wasn't the one who walked out. That it wasn't my decision to make."

She returned her full attention to Geoff.

"I'm not blaming you, Shona," he said. "I do wish we could go back a few months and retract some of our words."

She glanced once more into the crowd and saw Linda watching her from the third pew. It was impossible for Shona to read anything in the woman's enigmatic expression.

"Kemper seemed genuinely contrite about many things the night we talked," Geoff continued. "I believe you would have noticed a change in him had he lived."

She considered that for a moment. Was it possible that Dad had ended the relationship with Linda simply because he'd realized it was wrong?

"This time he sought God, Shona. When I resigned, I knew that only a miracle could change the direction Kemper MacDonald was going. When he approached me that night, he was riddled with guilt, and he even confessed some things he had done."

"Did he confess anything that might have a bearing on his murder?"

"No, but he did refer to a deal he had made that he intended to make right. That could very well have something to do with what happened to him. I've already spoken with the police about it."

"I think Dad might have needed you back on our team, Geoff, for some reason, and he knew the way to go about it." Again, she felt like a traitor, but she knew how her father had operated. "He had you fooled."

"Remember? I'm a cynic now. I've recently learned to expect the worst, so I wouldn't be disappointed."

"Maybe that's why you saw the worst in me," she said. "Because you expected it. I think there's power in a person's thoughts and words. If you expect the worst, you'll probably get it. The way you suspected me of lying Saturday night."

"I didn't suspect you of lying, but I felt you might have manipulated the facts—and in so doing, I felt as if you were manipulating me."

"That's called lying, Geoff," she snapped. How she would have loved to lose herself in his steady blue gaze. Instead, she was facing it down, as if she were facing a crowd of hostile politicians.

He was more willing to believe Dad than he was to believe his own wife.

"All I'm saying is that people change," he said. "*You've* changed."

"And you obviously don't like what you think I've become," she said, then held up her hand when he started to speak. "No, I'm not fishing for reassurance, I don't want to hear it."

Why should he forgive her? She was discovering, after all these months, that she had never forgiven herself.

"Shona?" His voice was tender, compassionate.

She took a deep breath. "Maybe we should just focus on the funeral today. It's about all I can handle."

She left him standing on the balcony as she went to join the rest of her family.

EIGHTEEN

As the minister eulogized Kemper MacDonald, Karah Lee felt as if her emotions had hardened to concrete. She didn't recognize the man being described. She doubted anyone had known that paragon of virtue.

She couldn't blame the minister, though. Shona had given him most of that information. Loving? Gentle?

What Karah Lee remembered was her father's behavior after he and her mother divorced. Soon after the divorce was final, Mom was diagnosed with pancreatic cancer. When Karah Lee quit college to take care of her mother, Kemper had tried to have her declared incompetent, in an attempt to force her back to the university. He had such high hopes for Karah Lee. She'd obviously been a disappointment to him.

After Mom's death, Karah Lee had difficulty getting into med school, at first, because of the record her father's manipulations had created. Just last year she'd discovered the way had been cleared because he'd pulled strings to make sure she got into the right school, received the right scholarship, possibly even the right residency.

It had undermined her confidence in her abilities. If her father had orchestrated her career, was she really a doctor? She knew better now, of course, and Dad had apologized.

Her long-held anger over his behavior had kept them apart even when he tried to make amends. How she wished now that she'd spoken with him then, when he'd wanted so badly to talk with her.

The question in her mind right now, though, was who else might hold a grudge against him because of something he had done in the past? How many others had he hurt in his climb to the top, in his need to control?

A slender hand slipped around her arm, and she glanced over to see Fawn looking up at her with concern.

Karah Lee would never be able to thank God enough for this teenager. Though she felt cut adrift from her own immediate family—of whom only Shona now remained, and a brother she knew superficially—she was amazed by the closeness she shared with this outspoken wild child.

Fawn wasn't nearly so wild these days; she was developing into a mature young woman. Granted, she still drove like a madwoman, but she would learn.

An arm wrapped around Karah Lee's shoulders from her other side, and she leaned into Taylor's muscular strength.

She needed that strength more than ever, especially now, when she was so vulnerable. She felt neither indomitable nor strong. She felt exposed in front of all these people, with the media looking on. Would Dad's killer strike again?

Shona sat motionless between Fawn and Geoff, listening to the minister's words. Could those words have been true, once upon a time? And maybe even more important, was it possible they might have become true in the future? Could Dad have experienced a change of heart, as Geoff assured her was the case?

Her conversation with Linda Plinkett continued to haunt her. What had Dad done that was so heinous that Linda refused to tell her about it before the funeral? Linda had suggested that Dad might have even killed himself, but the method of murder made that unlikely.

Yes, there had been times Dad drank too much, though not often. He liked to be in control, and alcohol robbed him of that control. When he was under the influence—something that hadn't happened in several weeks—he often expressed deep regret for past actions. But to kill himself over something he had done? Not Kemper MacDonald.

Shona glanced toward Jerrod, who had agreed to sit with the family. She had no doubt he was her brother, but he had not been raised in the family. His stepfather had been abusive and had eventually killed someone. What would that kind of influence have had on Jerrod over the years? What could he be hiding?

Even Karah Lee had harbored resentment toward Dad. How much resentment must Jerrod be dealing with? And what steps might he have been willing to take to appease that resentment?

Shona resisted the temptation to turn and study the other mourners—who possibly weren't all mourners. Some of these people might be gloating on the inside.

It was hard to imagine Wendy Phillips mourning Dad's death.

Irene's sorrow seemed sincere. She appeared teary-eyed since she'd arrived, but she was a good actress.

Mrs. Reynolds had come with her husband, and Shona had seen the genuine grief in the housekeeper's eyes. Mr. and Mrs. Reynolds weren't the only ones who had been affected by budget cuts.

Shona agreed with many of those cuts.

Even so, many objected. The question topmost on her mind—if someone had tried to make an example of Dad, would they also attempt to make one of her? Was it possible other lawmakers could be targets, as well?

After the interment at the cemetery, Geoff stood in the grass slightly apart from the lingering crowd, watching Shona, and surreptitiously checking to see if anyone else might be watching her.

Paul Forester approached her and drew her aside,

and Geoff guessed he was probably warning her to be cautious. Would she listen to Paul any more than she listened to anyone else?

"Geoff Tremaine?" came a male voice from behind him. He turned to find tall, dark-haired, sober-eyed Jerrod Houston standing beside him.

"Shona tells me Kemper talked to you about me." Jerrod had a deep voice, though he was soft-spoken.

Geoff held out his hand. "That's right, we're related. Welcome to the family. Once you get over all the awkwardness, you'll find we're truly a neurotic bunch."

Jerrod took the hand and shook. He had a firm grip, but not too firm. A faint smile touched his mouth. "You're the famous television personality of the family. Doesn't sound neurotic to me."

"You really do need to get to know us better, don't you? I'm glad you were able to make it today. It's quite a drive from Olathe."

"Two hours isn't bad. Did Kemper tell you how he and I first met?"

Geoff sobered. "Yes, he did."

"Karah Lee called me Saturday night and asked me about the medical files." He glanced toward those who continued to linger around Kemper's casket, keeping his voice low. "I needed some information about family medical history for a checkup I was having. I know I should have come right out and asked, but a guy doesn't just introduce himself to family who didn't know he existed, then start asking personal questions."

"I understand what you're saying, but typically, a man doesn't introduce himself to family and then hack into their medical files when they aren't looking."

"He might if his life could depend on what he found there."

"Such as?"

"Blood type for a possible bone marrow match. It was preliminary research to see if I needed to even bother anyone about it."

"Did you find what you needed?"

"My father matched. I know it was selfish of me, but I asked him not to share this with anyone else. I would probably have connected with them anyway, but I sought them out specifically because I needed help. I have leukemia."

"But now your father is dead."

Jerrod's gaze flicked from the crowd to Geoff. "Not completely."

"You mean Kemper already gave you bone marrow?"

Jerrod nodded. "He saved my life. The cancer is in remission." Again, he surveyed the crowd, his gaze lingering first on Shona, then on Karah Lee. "Did he...did my father tell you anything else about me?"

"He was proud of you," Geoff said. "In fact, discovering your existence seemed to change his outlook."

A smile touched Jerrod's face.

Shona glanced toward them, then said something to Paul, gave him a hug, and came toward them. "So you've met," she said when she'd reached them. "I think in the weeks ahead we need to gradually introduce you to the rest of the family, Jerrod."

"You mean there's more than this?" He gestured to the crowd that was now gradually dispersing to their cars.

"No, but we haven't introduced you. I've had a couple of cousins ask me who you were, but I haven't explained the situation yet."

"Is there a reason to do that? I didn't come looking for an extended family."

"Well, you got one, anyway."

"I'm not sure how the truth would go over right now. It'll only cause a disruption in everyone's life."

"What's life without a little disruption?" Shona asked. "It's still possible to get to know your sisters, your aunts, uncles, cousins, the whole clan. How about it? The church is serving a meal for us."

"Not today. I don't think that—"

"It isn't as if we have to make some big announcement, but you can mingle. You don't have to drive back to Olathe immediately, do you?" she asked.

Jerrod's gaze wavered. He glanced at his watch. "Actually, I should be going now. It's a long drive, and I need to get some work done tonight."

"But you have to eat," Shona protested.

"I'll grab a sandwich on the way." He gave her and

Geoff an awkward nod, then stopped and tapped on Karah Lee's shoulder on his way to his car, said another obviously brief goodbye, and left.

"What is up with him?" Shona asked softly.

"He's simply a shy computer programmer from Kansas who is overwhelmed by a new family. Give him time."

Shona glanced toward her father's black enamel casket, and Geoff heard her soft, broken sigh. She hadn't cried throughout the service—not in public. But the heartbreak was evident in those deep eyes.

"He knew you loved him, Shona. And he loved you more than you think."

"Where is he now?" she asked, her quiet voice charged with grief.

"I believe he's in heaven waiting for us."

NINETEEN

Darkness hovered in the storm clouds that crept over the city from the west early Monday evening. The weather forecast called for storms for the next several hours, but Shona knew it would do no good to try to convince Karah Lee to spend the night at the mansion now that it was cleared. She was determined to drive home. She had to work tomorrow.

Shona stepped out onto the circle drive in front of the house with Karah Lee. "Where's Fawn?"

"She's still in the kitchen with Mrs. Reynolds, waiting for something called a travel package."

"You'll eat well tonight."

"What's a travel package?"

"Our housekeeper is famous for her barbeque brisket sandwiches on homemade rolls. Her package will include fruit and giant chocolate-chip cookies and thermoses of iced tea."

Karah Lee whistled. "She doesn't spoil you much, does she?"

The sarcasm was obviously intended to be light-hearted, but Shona had felt edgy all afternoon, and the words struck a wrong chord. "Around here, that kind of thing isn't an indulgence, it's a necessity. I've been so busy this past year I've barely had time to eat a proper meal, much less prepare one."

"Well, then, you've been too busy," Karah Lee said.

Shona cut her a sharp glance. "Since when did you become my monitor?"

"What did Dad do, just dump all the work on you when Geoff resigned?"

"He hired extra office help."

"Ah, yes. He hired someone to do the busywork and left you with all the responsibility. That's great on a marriage."

Shona glared at her sister. "Our father's funeral was today," she snapped. "Can't you lay off?"

"I just thought a little reality might be nice for once," Karah Lee snapped back. "If someone were to judge by that eulogy you wrote, they might think our father was a paragon of virtue. You do realize that wasn't true, don't you?"

"Oh, sure, like Mom was a saint, but you didn't hear me ridiculing her behavior the day of her funeral."

"You've more than made up for that little slip over the years," Karah Lee said.

"All right! Catfight!" came a youthful voice from the veranda.

They both turned to find Fawn coming down the

broad steps to the circle drive, carrying a large plastic container.

"And here I thought you two were doing so well," Fawn said as she opened the back door and deposited her container.

Shona swallowed, ashamed of herself. She had almost protested that Karah Lee had started it. Fine example of statesmanship in action.

"Shona, there's no reason for you to stay here," Karah Lee said. "If the governor wants to reach you, he can get you on your cell phone."

"I misplaced it today, remember?"

"When did you do that?"

"I turned it off just before the service began and when I went to turn it back on, it wasn't in my purse. I asked you if you'd seen it. I asked everyone. No one had."

"So get a replacement."

"I will."

"And come stay with us for a few days."

"I can't leave the city. I'm still under suspicion."

"But you don't have to stay here, do you?" Karah Lee asked, her arms sweeping the house in a broad gesture. "You just have to tell the police where you're going."

"The FBI has officially taken over the case. I just want to settle back in now that they've cleared the house, okay? Don't worry, the security codes have been changed, and I'm safe. Mrs. Reynolds will be staying tonight—not that I asked her to, but she's as protective as the rest of you."

"As she should be, Aunt Shona," Fawn said.

Shona put her arm around the girl. "Aren't you the one who's always talking about faith? Where's yours?" She felt like a hypocrite, but she wasn't claiming faith, she was just demanding that someone who did claim faith actually proved it was there somewhere.

"Karah Lee's best friend, Bertie Meyer, says you're not supposed to tempt God," Fawn said. "Which means you should take precautions and not expect your guardian angels to do all the work."

Shona squeezed Fawn's shoulders again, wishing the girl didn't have to leave. "I'll surprise you someday and visit Hideaway," she said. "Have a safe trip."

She watched them go with a mixture of relief and regret. For a while this weekend, it had looked as if she and Karah Lee might be able to spend a whole day together without fighting—much. Still, maybe there was hope.

Seconds after she stepped into the vast entryway, Mrs. Reynolds came to her with the cordless phone, eyes wide with excitement.

"It's the governor!" she whispered.

Shona caught her breath silently, struggling to convey a confidence she didn't feel.

She accepted the phone. "Hello, sir, this is Shona Tremaine. Thank you again for attending the funeral today. How may I help you this evening?"

"Hello, Shona," came the familiar voice she had heard so often. There was a pause. "I'm sorry about this. I was going to wait until tomorrow to break the news, but I want you to hear it from me and not someone else."

She held her breath.

"I have no doubt that you would be the best choice to fill the vacancy that has been created by your father's tragedy."

She started breathing again. "Thank you."

"I know you've worked beside him tirelessly. He often commented to me about how glad he was to have you. That's why I'm so very sorry to have to tell you this, but I've appointed retired Senator John Harmon to serve as interim in Kemper's place until a special election can be held."

The breath hissed out of her as a last thread of hope broke in silence. In spite of what she'd told Geoff during the interview, she had little faith she'd win in an election after being overlooked for this appointment, especially considering the bad publicity that was circulating about her.

She swallowed hard. "I see. May I ask what guiding principle you were using for this decision?"

"You may ask anything you want. Due to the nature of your father's death and the questions that continue to linger in the minds of the authorities and the public, my advisors and I felt John would be a prudent choice."

"You mean because he isn't a suspect." She hadn't meant to make the statement aloud, but it was the truth.

"Again, I'm sorry for the way this has turned out."

Shona wasn't sure she was sorry. "Thank you for calling me. When will the announcement be made?"

"I have a press conference in about thirty minutes. I'll make it then."

"I'll be prepared."

"You will run in the next election, won't you? After all this is cleared up?"

"It's a possibility, but I can't say at this point."

"Let me know if there's anything I can do to help."

"Thank you, sir. I will."

After saying a respectful goodbye, Shona slumped into the cushioned velvet chair in the great marble entryway. She was sure that if she listened carefully, she could hear the inner crash of her dreams—of her whole life—collapsing around her.

Her father—the one person who had depended on her, and whom she had planned to disappoint—was dead. Murdered. Her husband, over whom she had planned to disappoint her father, obviously didn't trust her.

Had she really been on the verge of giving up her whole life for a man who no longer cared for her? Why?

She glanced up the curved stairway. Mrs. Reynolds would be out of earshot—she never eavesdropped on conversations. She would, however, be very curious about the outcome of this phone call.

Shona refused to cry. Instead, she returned the phone to its base, then found Mrs. Reynolds watching television in the rear guest room, where she had planned to stay the night.

"Mrs. Reynolds, go on home to your husband. I'll be fine by myself. I don't need a babysitter now."

The housekeeper's hazel eyes narrowed with concern. "Is everything okay?"

"Well, I won't be taking Dad's place, if that's what you mean. I'm still under suspicion, and the governor has decided it wouldn't be wise to appoint a suspect to a political position." She kept the bitterness from her voice. She couldn't blame the police and FBI for searching for Dad's killer, and she couldn't blame the governor for being cautious.

"I'm so sorry," Mrs. Reynolds said. "I still don't think you'll want to stay here alone. It's no problem for me to—"

"Your first priority is to your husband, and I know he's struggling with that new medication. Go ahead home. I'm a big girl, and there'll be no reason for anyone to want to harm me now, if they ever did. I'm not a threat to anyone. The governor will be making the announcement in thirty minutes."

Still, Mrs. Reynolds hesitated until Shona insisted. She needed solitude, and even though that wasn't difficult to find in this elegant monstrosity Dad had always been so proud of, she knew the housekeeper would be happier in her own home.

Finally, after Shona's instructions to take the rest of the week off, the woman left.

Shona was alone.

Karah Lee sat in the passenger seat with her feet firmly on the floor, hands in her lap, mouth shut tightly against her tendency to backseat drive. Fawn was doing a great job.

"Is it my imagination or are you driving more slowly than usual?"

"It's your imagination, of course. I've always been an excellent driver."

Karah Lee chuckled. "Fine. Be that way."

"I know something you don't know."

"Please don't tell me my slip was showing all through the funeral."

"Of course not. I would have told you that. I did some snooping today. I think I should become a private investigator."

"What did you find out?"

"Uncle Jerrod's hiding something. Linda Plinkett isn't getting along with Paul Forester. And I don't think the governor is going to appoint Shona in Kemper's place."

Karah Lee gaped at the girl. "Where did you dig all that up?"

Fawn shrugged, her face pensive in the deepening twilight as droplets of rain scattered across the windshield. "You'd be amazed what people will let slip to a friendly teenager. And I'm good at reading body language."

"What do you think Jerrod is hiding?"

"I think he knew Kemper better than he says he did. He was a lot more upset about your dad's death than he's letting on. He was trying hard not to cry all through the service."

"Maybe he's just sentimental."

"Don't forget the body language thing, Mom."

Karah Lee was always touched by that special word. She loved when this child of her heart called her mom. "Okay, well, I had hoped he would hang around and visit so I could grill him, but he said I could talk to Geoff if I had any questions. You know how some guys won't bare their souls to women. What about Linda and Paul?"

"Well, first of all, they passed right by each other in the vestibule of the church without speaking, and when Linda was seated in the auditorium, Paul saw where she sat and changed directions. I watched them."

"Okay, so there's bad blood amongst the task force."

"Is the FBI investigating them?" Fawn asked.

"Both of them were questioned, as well as Mrs. Reynolds and her husband, the gardener, Mr. Rice, and the rest of the office staff."

"What about the guy who Kemper argued with a few weeks ago?" Fawn asked.

"What guy?"

"Kemper had some remodeling done on three of

the guest rooms and the bathrooms downstairs at the mansion. The guy gave a quote, then changed his mind halfway through and doubled the price, even though he had a contract."

"Shona told you all that?"

"Of course not. I was eavesdropping on those three sweet old women who worked on Kemper's last campaign."

"You eavesdrop?"

"It's the best way to get good information. Anyway, this remodeling guy ran out of money, couldn't get the work done, and your dad fired him and sued, then hired someone else to take care of it and fix the damage the first guy did."

"So that first guy was likely mad at Dad."

"I'd say. I think we've got our work cut out," Fawn said.

"What do you mean we?"

"Well, the FBI isn't finding much yet, and Shona is in their crosshairs. Looks like she could use some help." Fawn slowed, entering the city limits of Lake of the Ozarks. "Speaking of which, the reason I don't think Shona's getting the appointment is because the governor looked too uncomfortable when the reporters ask him point-blank about it after the service. Shona's going to feel pretty bad."

"Maybe that'll convince her to come to Hideaway for a few days, at least."

"But why should she?" Fawn asked. "If she isn't

going to be in the power position, she isn't a threat to anyone."

Karah Lee rode in silence as the lights of the lake town flashed through the car. "We'll just have to wait and see what she decides to do for herself. She's a big girl."

Fawn sighed heavily. "She's all alone now. Not even Geoff is close to her."

"I suppose you eavesdropped on that conversation, as well?"

"Didn't have to. I could see it in their eyes, in the stiffness in their shoulders when they were together, in their overly bright smiles. Nothing like you and Taylor, all weird about each other."

"We're not weird."

"Goopy weird."

"Anyway, we'll need to do some extra praying for Shona until she gets over this."

TWENTY

The mansion had become a prison. Shona couldn't remember when that had happened, but she knew she'd been fighting this sensation for weeks. In all the excitement, tragedy and pain of the past few days, that hadn't changed. She didn't feel safe here, she felt incarcerated.

Since Mrs. Reynolds left twenty minutes ago, the windows seemed to be watching her. Even though she completely avoided the office where she had found Dad, she still felt as if something hovered in the air—some dark memories that would haunt her as surely as any ghost. She had never believed in ghosts, but she knew better than to dismiss the obvious presence of evil in the world.

She knew the security was in place. No one could reach her here—and no one was going to try. Whatever the killer had against Dad, the whole state would know in just a few moments that she wasn't a threat to anyone.

She took a brisket sandwich from the refrigerator—Mrs. Reynolds made the best in the world—and poured a glass of milk, then carried the food upstairs on a tray to her suite in the west wing.

She had a small fridge in the spacious sitting room, and often stayed here in the evenings, reading reports, surfing the Web for the latest developments around the state and country. This was where she had spent so much of her time these past months…since leaving Geoff. It was where she'd buried herself.

As she set her tray on the coffee table, she felt a chill. No matter where she went in the house, she couldn't escape Dad's presence—and the reminders. The longer she stayed here, the more oppressive this place felt.

It wasn't until the rich tones of the grandfather clock on the second-floor landing struck eight that she gave up her game of make-believe. She couldn't stay.

She was packed in less than ten minutes, driving her Escalade through the open garage door in twelve. All the alarms were activated, the answering machine and call forwarding set, though it wouldn't do much good to have call forwarding when she didn't have a phone to receive calls. She would buy a new cell phone tomorrow.

It didn't matter, anyway. Why would she receive any calls?

Before she could indulge in any more self-pity, she pressed the garage door remote and drove around the side of the house. The street was deserted. Instead of turning in the direction of the Capitol Plaza, she turned left and drove to the cemetery.

In all the busyness of her life, she'd had so little time to become lonely. Until now.

Now the sensation was an oppressive weight that threatened to crush her.

Geoff sat in Wendy's office, once again an unwilling recipient of her close scrutiny. "What's up this time, boss?"

"You did a passable interview with Shona Saturday night, no doubt about that, but we need more from you."

"Like what?"

"You could have asked a few more leading questions. We need to strike while we have the public's attention. When can you get another interview with her?"

"I can't."

"Why not?"

"First of all, because I don't want to intrude on her grief again. Second, because I think it's sensationalism to make a media circus out of a murder."

Wendy sat back in her plush leather chair and fingered a paperclip on her desk while the chatter and laughter in the other rooms drifted through her closed door. She liked to use this tactic, let her prey wonder what was on her mind.

It wasn't working on Geoff. He was pretty sure he

already knew what she was thinking. He stood up. "If that's all you wanted, it's been a long day, and I'd—"

"I'm putting you on probation, Mr. Tremaine."

He closed his eyes and nodded. It was what he'd expected. She had a job to do, and he couldn't do what she had asked.

"You do realize, don't you," he said, "that because of the interview last Saturday, Shona could be in danger?"

Wendy waved that statement away irritably. "We just got the announcement from the governor. She's not a threat to anyone. I think you need a break. Megan's replacing you this next week so you'll have some downtime."

"Do what you have to." He reached for the door.

"I'm not bluffing this time, Geoff. Your refusal to work with me could cost you your job."

He didn't stop.

"You don't have your father-in-law to fall back on, Tremaine!" she called after him, her voice echoing off the walls and carrying down the corridor.

When he reached his dressing room he turned on his cell phone. Another text message awaited him. It was another Bible devotional from Kemper.

And yet it wasn't. All Kemper had sent him had been the address of a Scripture passage, John 2:14, and the words *Love is the key.*

Gooseflesh pricked the back of his neck. This was getting too strange. He knew text messages could be programmed to arrive at certain times, and that Kemper had recently learned some things from his son, but why this?

"Lord, what am I missing? Please, help me understand. What was Kemper trying to tell me?" It obviously wasn't a typical Bible study, because the verses were out of context and made no point. Could Kemper have suspected his life might be in danger?

There was something niggling at the back of Geoff's mind. The first message he'd received had been about Moses being hidden in the bull rushes.

Moses…the baby.

Geoff sighed and shook his head. Was he reading something into this that wasn't there?

Baby…Kemper had said something to Shona about getting the little one out.

Shona's baby was her PDA. Just today, her cell phone had turned up missing.

What if someone had been trying to get to her PDA to see what might be on it?

But who would do that unless someone thought there might be something there to find? Kemper had mentioned his deal with the devil. Could he have hidden some information in Shona's PDA for safekeeping, then left a trail for Geoff to follow in case anything happened?

Shona still had that PDA. If someone close to her had picked up on Kemper's final words…the little one…then Shona could be in danger right now.

This final message was obvious. Somehow, Kemper was giving them a password, or the location of a password. 2:14 would be February 14, Valentine's Day, when Geoff and Shona had been married. Love is the key. He needed to check her calendar.

He needed to talk to Shona. He pressed speed dial. No answer. He dialed the mansion. The answering machine picked up.

"Shona, this is Geoff. If you're there, pick up the phone, please." He waited, knowing she might be screening all calls. "Shona? This is serious. Answer if you're there."

Nothing.

He grabbed his jacket, shoved his cell phone into his pocket and removed a few personal items from the dressing room, including his laptop. If Wendy decided to fire him next week, he didn't want the ignominy of doing the cleanout later.

Now he had more important things to do. He needed to get to Shona.

Lightning flashed along the forest top, placing the trees into sepia relief, like a photographic negative backlit by the sun. A stiff, wet breeze rustled the new leaves and played at Shona's hair.

She knelt at the foot of the grave, nearly overwhelmed by the scent of the flowers stacked atop the mound that covered her father.

"Dad, I wish I knew what you were up to. I wish

you'd told me." She realized there must have been much he hadn't shared with her. Obviously, he'd told Geoff things he'd never told her.

In spite of his dependence on her help, Dad had been a staunch member of the "good ol' boys" club, with old-school ideas about a woman's role. He never liked to worry her about anything he knew she didn't approve of, anyway. Of course, he must have realized his actions had often caused distress to the women in his life, his daughters and wives. He had apologized to Shona once for divorcing her mother, and then never said another word about it.

"To someone, you were the enemy," she murmured, then glanced around her, feeling silly for talking to a pile of flowers. "I just wish you'd told me more."

Something moved in the depths of the trees to her left. She stiffened. Another sudden breeze whipped past her, and she relaxed.

When the movement of wind in the trees made her nervous, it was time for a reality check. She hadn't seen anyone following her here, and though she hadn't been paying particular attention, it had long ago become her habit to keep an eye on traffic around her. The media could be intrusive and vicious.

She picked up a white rose from the assortment of blooms, and held it to her face. All weekend, she had half expected Dad to come stalking up to her and ask why she wasn't at work, or tell her one of his corny jokes, or advise her of a change of plans.

Sitting at his grave, she realized, in the silence, that he was gone for good.

"Where are you, Dad?" she whispered. "Did you really have a change of heart?" She glanced up into the roiling dark clouds. What was past them? Something, she knew. Mom had always believed so passionately about the God she served. Mom had served imperfectly, but she had believed, of that Shona had no doubt. Geoff believed, and Karah Lee and Fawn.

"Everyone but me, it seems."

A glow flickered in the corner of her vision, and she looked around quickly. Lightning, perhaps?

"I just wish I knew what you were trying to tell me Friday night." She had figured out what he meant by "shot," but why did he want her away from Jefferson City? Did he mean he had wanted her out of politics? Was he referring to his wish that she and Geoff would get back together?

And the reference to her little one…had that been the ravings of a man hallucinating? He'd said, "You need your little one…get…away."

"What little one, Dad? What were you trying to tell me?"

The first fat drops of rain fell on her hands and face. She wrapped her blazer more tightly around her as she stood.

"I'll miss you, Dad," she whispered, and she definitely would. No one else had needed her as much as he had. No one else had trusted her, either, obviously.

Shaking away another attack of grief, she rushed to her vehicle and climbed inside. Her purse had fallen from the seat to the floor, and she bent to retrieve it.

Her PDA slid out, and she reached to pick it up.

A *thud-crack-thud-crack* startled her, and she straightened. Sheet lightning raced across the sky before her. Then she saw something else. The lightning illuminated a spider-web tracing of glass that had shattered outward from a hole in the windshield. Directly in front of her.

Someone had shot at her.

Geoff pulled into the drive in front of the MacDonald mansion, frustrated that Shona continued to ignore his messages. A quick call to Mrs. Reynolds had revealed that Shona had sent home the housekeeper and given her the rest of the week off. But why? Shona only did that when she was planning to travel.

She must be devastated about the governor's appointment. She'd pinned her hopes on taking her father's place, not so much because she loved the limelight and the glory. She didn't. But that connection to her father was important.

Yes, she felt strongly about doing her best for the good of Missouri. She truly believed in her life's calling. But right now, on the evening of her father's funeral, Geoff knew she had needed that connection to Kemper.

Had she been so tired and discouraged that she'd already gone to bed this early?

Once again, he pressed speed dial and waited. When the machine picked up, he disconnected. The security company had changed all the codes. He didn't know what they were now. Once upon a time he'd known them by heart.

That depressed him.

But what disturbed him the most right now was the conviction that no one was in that house.

Where would Shona have gone?

He got out of the car. Rain drenched him as he ran up to the broad, covered veranda. The security lights made the falling drops glow in the dark, as if the clouds had taken a hit of phosphorescence.

He rang the doorbell and pounded on the heavy mahogany wood of the door.

No light twinkled on in the house. No reply on the speaker beside the threshold.

Shona sat staring out the cracked windshield, gripped by terror, fury and astonishment that someone would be so brazen.

And yet, she was exposed out here in the middle of the cemetery in the middle of a storm in the darkness, with no way to call for help.

She started the Escalade and shoved it into Reverse. When she turned on the headlights, a *thud-crack* snapped against the windshield on the passenger side.

She shoved the gear into Drive and tromped on the accelerator, keeping her head low.

She had to get out of here.

TWENTY-ONE

Karah Lee was as close to the edge of a doze as she'd ever been with Fawn behind the steering wheel. She'd have been out to the world in seconds if her cell phone hadn't chirped and brought her to consciousness. She snuffled and straightened, then fumbled for the phone. She discovered she was sitting on the thing.

It was Geoff. "Karah Lee, have you heard from Shona?"

"Not since we left her in Jeff City less than an hour ago. Why?"

"Did she say anything about where she intended to go tonight?"

"I had the impression she would be staying home, waiting for the governor to call. You know she lost her cell phone today, and she sure didn't want to miss that call."

"The announcement has been made," Geoff said. "Shona will not be filling Kemper's position. I need to find her as soon as possible."

Karah Lee sat up straighter, alerted by the tone of his voice. "What are you thinking?"

"I'm thinking she could be in danger. That PDA of hers could have some information on it that could be dangerous to her, and she keeps it with her all the time."

Karah Lee hated the tension that curled through her insides like electrified wire. There was no reason for it, of course. Geoff was worrying for nothing. Wasn't he?

"What's happening?" Fawn asked.

"I'm not sure," Karah Lee said to the girl, then into the phone, "Geoff, if you think there's a problem, why don't you call the police?"

"I have, and the FBI. I thought I'd call you. I haven't been able to raise her at the house, and I wondered if she might possibly be with you, or if she'd told you where she planned to go this evening."

"No, Geoff. She wouldn't budge when we tried to get her to come to Hideaway with us. Big sister doesn't feel comfortable spending time with little sister." Karah Lee heard the bitterness in her voice and instantly regretted her tone.

"We're coming back," she said.

"No. You don't need to be here, you need to be safely at home, and it wouldn't hurt to take some safety precautions there, as well. Just keep your line open so I can call you for updates."

"You'd better believe it."

"And if by chance she does call you, tell her to contact me immediately."

"Have you checked to see if her car is in the garage?"

"I don't have access anymore. Mrs. Reynolds is on her way over with a key, and as I said, I've called the FBI."

"I thought Mrs. Reynolds was going to spend the night."

"Shona apparently wanted to be alone after she got the bad news."

"Figures." Karah Lee braced herself as Fawn took a curve too sharply. "Geoff, I remember the day of Mom's funeral, after everyone went home and I was all alone at the house, I couldn't stay there. I went back to the cemetery. No one else had ever loved me the way my mother did, and I just couldn't let her go."

"You think Shona went to the cemetery?"

"It's possible."

"I'll check it out and call you when I know something."

"Thanks. Meanwhile, we'll be praying."

Headlights glared in Shona's rear-view mirror. She floored the accelerator, gripping the steering wheel as she swerved to avoid a limb in the road. Her pursuer was gaining on her rapidly, and the country road was deserted at this time of evening.

A low branch slapped her windshield. She cried out as if someone had shot through the window again. As she drew near the bank of the Missouri River, the vehicle—a large vehicle—drew up behind her so closely she feared it would ram her from behind.

Instead, it pulled to the side of Shona's car, trying to draw abreast. She tromped into passing gear and shot forward. The other car rammed her back fender. The steering wheel jerked in her hand, and she saw the glow of city lights against the surface of the water, reflecting from the other side of the river.

The lunatic was trying to force her over the bank!

She jerked the wheel back, not caring if she destroyed her vehicle as long as she stayed out of the river.

The other car rammed her again. The front grill of the Escalade struck sparks off the metal barrier fence between Shona's car and the river's edge.

Her wheels sunk into a bog, and she pressed harder on the accelerator, spinning mud in every direction as she fishtailed away. As she picked up speed, the headlights behind her receded. She plunged into the night, her fingers stiff on the steering wheel, her body taut with terror.

Dad was right. She had to get out of Jefferson City. In fact, she was already out, and she couldn't afford to return.

She no longer knew whom she could trust.

Karah Lee and Fawn were on I-44 headed west when Geoff called again.

"Mrs. Reynolds met me at the house and we checked the garage. Shona took the Escalade."

"So she could be anywhere."

"I'm on my way to the cemetery. The police aren't too happy with me, but I'm not exactly thrilled with them right now, either. I'll be in touch."

Lightning flashed. From the corner of her eye, Shona caught the shape of an SUV in her side window seconds before it drew even and rammed into her front bumper. A Hummer. Paul?

No!

It hit her again. She screamed and slammed her brakes to keep from plunging over the cliffs ahead. She shoved the gear into Reverse, but the Hummer shadowed her.

Another bolt of lightning highlighted the driver of the other car—and the outline of a gun aimed at her. The shock of recognition robbed her of the ability to think—or to react. There was another crack of glass, and she screamed. "Uncle Paul!"

She floored it and fishtailed away, her rear tire dropping hard over the side of a table of rock. Paul's taillights lunged at her. A clamor of metal against metal echoed in her ears as she felt herself rolling with the momentum of the Escalade, tumbling down the hillside toward the Missouri River.

Geoff raced through the darkness as he dialed Linda Plinkett's number. She answered on the first ring. She sounded hoarse and nasal, as if she'd been crying.

"Linda, I need to ask you something."

"And what would that be?"

"I heard a wild tale about Kemper and Kristin."

"Oh, don't tell me that stupid rumor is still circulating," she snapped.

"So it's just a rumor?"

"Of course it is. Kristin is sixteen. She's not going to be interested in a sixty-year-old man, no matter how attractive he is to her mother. And he never had to resort to forcing himself on women. That's just sick."

"Kristin isn't pregnant?"

There was a long pause. "Yes, as a matter of fact, she is, but that misfortune happened while she was on the French Riviera last December with her father, not here in Jefferson City."

"Paul told me about it."

There was a sharp intake of breath. "Why would he say something like that?"

"That was what I wondered. A man who prides himself on his reputation for honesty wouldn't go around spreading rumors like that unless he knew it to be true, or unless he was desperate to deflect attention from himself. But what would he want deflected?"

"And what good would it do to send someone on a wild-goose chase if it was just temporary?" Linda asked. "You were bound to discover soon enough that what he told you was a lie."

"So he's buying time," Geoff said. "But for what?"

There was a pause. "Did you tell the police what Paul said?"

"Yes, but I also told them what you said about Paul. I started to wonder about him. You've said often enough that he has this need to be in control, and yet Kemper took control when he joined the task force. Kemper and Paul are friends, but Paul was the one who first suggested the campaign slogan 'Stop bleeding Missouri dry.'"

"Kemper took that from him. It didn't make Paul happy, but he didn't say much about it. Still, I can't imagine that it would make him angry enough to kill Kemper."

"What would?"

"I don't know. Whatever it might be, I can't see Paul killing in a fit of passion. Kemper's murder was premeditated. Cold. There's something else going on we don't know about. I've always believed Paul's quest for honesty took second place to his need for control. When Kemper entered the political arena, his natural charisma shot him to the top of the popularity polls."

"Did Paul seem upset about that?"

"Paul was ecstatic. That was when he started talking about Kemper running for governor, and he hoped he'd be lieutenant governor. Shona was in their sights for Kemper's position."

"Linda, Shona is the reason I'm calling you. I can't find Shona. She isn't at the house, and I'm on my way to the cemetery at Karah Lee's suggestion."

"Why are you worried?"

"Something Kemper said just occurred to me. He said something to Shona about getting the 'little one' out. Shona thought he was hallucinating by then, but now I wonder. She carries her cell phone and her PDA in her purse at all times. Kemper always teased Shona about taking such good care of her little computer. He called it her 'baby.' Babies are often called little ones. What if there's incriminating evidence there?"

"But the police would have any information Kemper would have left on his home office computer."

"Not if the information was only on Shona's PDA. I've been getting some strange text messages that make me think Kemper might have placed something there for safekeeping. Someone took Shona's cell phone during the funeral service or soon after. What if that was a mistake? What if they meant to take the PDA?"

"But how would anyone know he had stored information there?" Linda asked. "You're just guessing at this."

"I'm not guessing anymore, Linda, it just takes me a while to work out a word puzzle."

"Or to convince yourself such a thing exists."

"Listen to me for a moment. Kemper's first posthumous message to me was about Moses being hidden in the bullrushes when he was a baby."

"You're sure that actually came from Kemper?"

"I had been receiving other messages from him when he was alive. He was studying his Bible and sharing some of the things he learned with me, so yes, I believe this came from Kemper. He knew how to send delayed messages. He learned this from Jerrod."

"But what was the significance of this particular message?"

"Moses was a baby in this story. That's significant if you consider Shona's baby was her PDA, according to Kemper." The more Geoff thought about it, the more it made sense.

"I think you're stretching things beyond the point of recognition."

"Bear with me a moment. Someone asked Kemper one day during an interview why he wanted to run for governor."

"I remember that," Linda said softly. "He said, 'Governor? I want to be king!' Shona nearly brained him."

"Pharoah's daughter took Moses. Pharoah was a king."

There was a sigh. "Okay, so you're saying that since Shona's baby is her PDA, Kemper might have been telling you he had encoded some message there that was important?"

"That's what I'm saying. He sent me other scripture passages that might be the key, but I wonder what kind of information he might have hidden there, and why."

"And who would know him well enough to

guess what he had done?" Linda asked. "And why encode messages?"

"Maybe he was being watched closely by someone who knew him well," Geoff said. "Any ideas?"

There was a long silence, then a sigh. "Maybe. I knew Kemper and Paul were working on their war chest. They were making some substantial gains on it until two weeks ago, when Kemper decided to make this big, crazy turnaround in his life. We had some information a few weeks ago that was pure gold about a major meth lab on someone's private land, and I wondered why we had heard nothing about a bust. Is it possible Kemper and Paul were protecting this lab for a fee?"

"For their war chest? Kemper alluded to something like that when he spoke with me. He said he'd made a deal with the devil."

"Is the devil after Shona now?"

Geoff shot into passing gear. "I'm going to find out."

A cold spray of water splashed against Shona's face, startling her back to consciousness. She was in the Escalade in the river, and she could feel the current pushing her.

She reached for the door handle, but the force of the water would not allow her to push the door open. She heard the sound of crackling glass as the pressure increased against the windshield.

She fumbled in the glove compartment for the

emergency life hammer device Geoff had placed in her car last year for safety. She drew her arm back and whacked the sharp metal end of the instrument against the glass of the driver's-side window. More water sprayed her in the face. She hit it again, and the river invaded with the force of an ocean wave, shoving her against the seat, shocking her with cold, taking her breath away.

Pushing off with her feet, she fumbled blindly for the escape hatch, and felt glass scraping against her arm.

Her blazer caught, and she let it slide from her shoulders. Finally she was free and floating in black wetness, confused, lost, not sure which way was up.

Her lungs ached for air as she stared through the blackness, searching for light. She needed to swim, needed to get to the surface.

Then she saw the rising bubbles, lit by the headlights that continued to glow from her SUV. She kicked, lungs near to bursting, fighting to not inhale.

Please, God, help me!

Just as she realized she could no longer hold off, her mouth opened, she gasped, and broke the surface.

Choking and spluttering, she studied her position, and saw the shoreline looming near. She was tempted to allow the current to carry her in, but she knew there was a killer somewhere nearby, possibly waiting for her to float into his grasp.

Oh, Uncle Paul. Why? She braced herself and

turned to stroke toward the far shoreline when she heard a splash nearby and felt a hand come down on her shoulder. Her scream burst across the night and echoed into the distance as she tried to swim away.

Paul Forester's meaty arm came around her waist and he pulled her in. "I'm sorry, sweetheart." His deep, guttural growl, always so familiar and trusted, now held only terror for her. "I tried everything I could to keep this from happening. If only I'd realized sooner…if only I'd known to stop all this before it happened."

"What are you talking about, Uncle Paul? What are you doing?" Her feet touched rocks, and she scrambled to get a footing—and leverage.

"Your father did some things. I should say, he and I did some things that we weren't proud of. And then he changed his mind. He wanted to confess everything to the police. He was crazy! I couldn't let him do that. We had much more than our careers at stake."

"I don't understand. Why do—"

"Where's the baby, Shona?"

"The baby? What are—"

"I need that computer!" His growl deepened. "It's the only place I haven't looked. Kemper had vital information hidden— Where is it?"

Geoff gripped the steering wheel so hard that he considered the possibility that he might crack it. His headlights probed the darkness ahead of him, and his gaze probed the darkness past the road, in the direction of the cemetery.

Karah Lee was right, Shona would most likely have gone to the cemetery. Though the two sisters fought whenever they were near each other, they were alike in so many ways. Shona had been given little time to grieve since her father's death. She would want to do that in private.

Someone who knew her well would know that, and possibly follow her out.

No other cars were on this country lane tonight. Overhanging trees pulsed the moonlight briefly as it peeked from between the clouds for a few seconds. A glint of something metallic caught his attention from the bank of the river. A large SUV was parked there, at a drunken angle, completely off the blacktop.

Lightning flashed, and he saw the vehicle more clearly. It wasn't Shona's Escalade. It was Paul's Hummer.

Paul Forester, who had lied to him about Linda to divert his attention.

Another flash of lightning showed him a nightmare scene, two forms standing in the river, like a hellish depiction of a baptism scene.

He slammed the brakes and swerved from the road. *Lord, protect her!*

Lightning flashed around them, and Shona had the fleeting impression that she and Paul stood in a river of liquid silver. She had to be dreaming. She would wake up any moment.

Yet Paul's grip on her arm felt real, and the shape of the pistol in his right hand looked solid.

"Paul, I don't know what you think I have, but you're so wrong. What's come over you?" As another flash revealed his expression once more, she glimpsed a hollow deadness in his eyes. And suddenly, she knew. No. It couldn't be.

"Dad," she whispered. "You killed Dad."

"He did it to himself." The strained voice didn't even sound like her beloved uncle Paul. When had everything changed?

"You're blaming Dad for forcing you to murder him?" she snapped. "You're the one with the medical training. You're the one with access to the house, and to the drugs. No one would ever suspect you." As she spoke, she thought she glimpsed a moving shape in the periphery of her vision, heard a scatter of small stones.

Paul's grip tightened, and as he turned toward the sound, Shona tried to lunge from his grasp.

There was a splash of water beside them. As the lightning flashed yet again, there was a look of pure agony in Paul's expression. His grip became a vice. Shona cried out and fought him, losing her footing on the slick rocks below.

"Shona!" came Geoff's frantic voice. "Get away!" He lunged between her and Paul, grappling for control of the weapon.

In the darkness, a blast tore through the night.

"Geoff!" she cried. "Geoff, what—"

There was a splash of water, and arms grabbed her. "It's okay," Geoff said. "Get back on shore. You don't need to see this."

She waited until another flash of lightning showed her what her husband didn't want her to see.

Paul Forester floated faceup, caught by the current of the river. The expression in his open eyes was lifeless, and the spatter of blood around the hole in his forehead told her more than she could stand.

He was dead.

"You shot him?" she asked, shivering in the suddenly chilly air.

"He never relinquished control of the gun," Geoff said. "He shot himself."

Geoff drew her close, and she allowed herself to be cradled in his strong, reassuring arms.

TWENTY-TWO

Shona sat in the lounger on the deck of Bertie Meyer's bed-and-breakfast in Hideaway on Friday morning. She felt as if she would never tire of the view from here—Table Rock Lake sparkling in the late morning sunshine, blooms of every description decorating the cliffs on the opposite shore. No wonder Karah Lee had rented her cottage here on the grounds.

A goat bleated from somewhere below, and a cat—Karah Lee's cat, Monster—answered.

Only in Hideaway.

Peace. How long had it been since she had felt this totally at peace?

She closed her eyes and listened to Karah Lee and Fawn bicker and was glad that, for once, her sister was squabbling with someone else.

Since arriving here three days ago, Shona had done nothing but sleep, eat, catch up on her reading, and sit on this deck, soaking up the peace. She had tried not to think about the horrors of the past week.

Mostly, she had succeeded. Every time she closed her eyes and caught an image of Uncle Paul's anguished expression in the flash of lightning, she prayed. She actually prayed.

Even more amazing to her, those prayers had been answered.

This sudden connection with God had happened gently, quietly. One moment she'd been struggling to put the past few days out of her mind, and the next, Karah Lee mentioned something about God's grace. That was when it had clicked for Shona. That was when she looked back over her life and recognized God's presence there, as if guarding her, drawing her to Him, always drawing.

All those years she'd sought to make the right choices in her life, and so often making the wrong ones, she could have done it so much more easily. And yet her self-sufficiency had gotten in the way, just as it had with Geoff last year.

It was in that one second of discovery that she became a believer. One moment, she was a woman on her own. The next, she was a woman filled with the joy of discovery, thanking God for a Christian mother who, although heavily flawed, had pointed her daughters in the right direction decades ago.

Whatever Shona's future held—and she had no idea what that might be, though she suspected it would be in the political arena—she knew she would never be alone again.

If only she had discovered this treasure last year before destroying the most important human relationship in her life. And yet, was it destroyed? Geoff had been so tender with her—and even now, as the media rocked with news of Paul's deception, Geoff avoided all public mention of Shona's name.

Uncle Paul had destroyed everything in his life, and Monday night he had destroyed himself. Dad had managed to communicate what was needed for Geoff to pull up information from her PDA—which was rescued on Wednesday from the depths of the Missouri River. Amazingly, the information Dad had hidden was enough to put away six members of a major drug ring for several years. They had been financing Dad's and Paul's campaign efforts—until Dad's change of heart.

"It should be this color, antique, with lots of lace and satin and beads," Fawn was insisting as she stepped to the edge of the deck and held out a swatch of fabric to Karah Lee.

"I'm supposed to wear white," Karah Lee said. "I've earned it."

"The antique will go better with your hair than white," Fawn said. "Besides, it's the antique that is supposed to signify virginal. The bright white signifies joy. I read that in one of my bride magazines."

"I like the white," Karah Lee said. "The brighter the better."

Fawn made a face. "Aunt Shona, can you beat

some sense into her? She's going to commit fashion suicide. There'll be a clash."

"I think there already is one," Shona said. "Why don't you let her have what she wants? It's her wedding. Then when you plan yours, she'll have to butt out and leave you to it."

Both women looked at her with expressions that showed they were less than enthusiastic about the idea.

"Here's an idea," Karah Lee said. "Taylor and I will elope. You'll all wake up one morning and we'll be gone, and when we return, we'll be Mr. and Mrs. Taylor Jackson. And everyone will thank us for sparing them the work and worry of another wedding in the community."

"Thank you?" Fawn exclaimed. "Hardly. This town doesn't have a lot of weddings, and everyone makes a party out of the least little celebration just because they're starving for some excitement. Don't rob everyone of their chance to party."

"Well, now." Shona stood up and stepped to the railing, gazing down toward the gazebos dotting the broad lawn by the municipal boat dock. "That sounds like an excellent idea. What this town needs is a wedding chapel."

"You think so?" Karah Lee asked. "We've already got three churches."

"Yes, but if you had a wedding chapel, that would draw even more tourists here from Branson. Think about it. Some wise individual could own the chapel, do all the planning, cake decorating, even have a shop offering wedding attire."

A voice spoke from behind them. "They could specialize in vow renewals." The voice was deep. It was male.

Shona turned and saw her husband standing in the doorway, his face lit by the sun, as those same beams caught his wavy, light brown hair and shot streaks of pale fire across it.

"Uncle Geoff!" Fawn rushed forward with a quick hug. "Why didn't you tell us you were coming?"

"Because I was afraid Shona might disappear again and I wanted to talk to her before she could get away."

"That's ridiculous, of course I wouldn't disappear," Shona told him. "Why would I do something like that?"

"Maybe because you're avoiding me? Maybe because you're retreating from the world right now?"

"I'm taking some much needed—and might I say, much deserved—vacation time. Had you wanted to contact me all you had to do was call my new cell phone."

"What I want to talk to you about is best done in person."

"Oh? Such as?"

"I wanted to know if you were recovering from the past week."

"I'm doing fine." She saw Karah Lee grab Fawn's arm and tug her into the house, then slide the glass door shut behind them.

"And how about the past year?" Geoff asked.

Shona looked up at him, puzzled. "The past year?"

"I know it's been difficult for you. I think you missed me almost as much as I missed you. I understand, from several sources, that you've blamed yourself for all the misunderstandings and battles between us."

"Haven't you?"

He gestured toward the deck chair she had so recently vacated, and when she returned to it, he took the one beside her. "At first I was so angry and stunned that I did blame you. That was last year, when I was young and callow."

"And now you're old and wise?" she asked dryly.

"Wiser than I was last year. Loneliness does that to a person. That, and nearly losing the person you love most in the whole world for the second time. I guess it takes that kind of shock to wake some people up."

She knew exactly what he meant, and she loved the words coming from his lips.

He leaned closer, and she could feel the warmth of his body, smell the clean scent of his cologne, could see the sunlight brightening his eyes.

"It was arrogant of me to think I could snap my fingers and you would quit your job, abandon your father and your service to the state. You truly are one of the rare public servants who believes in actually serving the public."

"Is this an apology?"

He nodded. "Will you forgive me? I was wrong."

"So was I. You were my husband, and I know there's a passage in the Bible that tells us to leave our parents and cleave to our spouse. That wasn't clear to me last year. Now it is."

"And what if your husband were to tell you that he has a new job? This one with a television station in Columbia?"

"I would say it's about time you gave Wendy your walking papers."

"And what if I were to tell you that I intend to stand with you if you decide to run for office next year?"

"What makes you think I'll want to run for office?"

"Because you were born to serve. You're a natural. You love this state, and you love this country, and that's where your heart will always be. I know, because it's where mine is. Why settle for state senate? You could go for the United States Senate."

"Hold it. I need some time to think about that. First, I need to focus on doing the right thing here and now."

He slipped to his knees in front of her. She laughed and tried to tug him up, but he wouldn't move.

"Shona Tremaine, will you marry me again? I love you. I've never stopped loving you, and my life is so empty without you in it."

"But we're still married. Why do you want to get married again?"

He rolled his eyes and leaned toward her, placing a hand on each arm of her chair, as if to guarantee she would not get away so easily this time. "Because I want to make those vows fresh. I want us to hold them in our hearts so we never forget them again, now that we understand what they truly mean. I want to publicly state that we belong to one another, so there will be no question in anyone's mind."

She wrapped her arms around his neck and drew him to her. The lips she had longed for all these months molded so perfectly to hers, so warm and assuring. The arms that she had ached for drew her against him. This was where she had always belonged. Now, finally, she was home again.

* * * * *

Turn the page for a sneak peek of
Hannah Alexander's next Hideaway novel,
GRAVE RISK
available from Steeple Hill books
in January 2007.

Saturday afternoon, Sept. 3

Fingers touched Jill Cooper's face and marched across her cheekbones like a troop of spiders. She cringed and caught her breath.

She couldn't do this. She wanted to shrink from the intrusion, or jump up from this table and escape this place. What horrors lay behind those other doors? What had she allowed herself to be talked into?

"Too rough?" Sheena Marshall had a bright, perky voice that grated. All the employees of this spa—except for Mary Marshall, Sheena's mother—seemed to have issues with terminal optimism.

"It's fine." Jill wanted to ask her when the sheets had last been washed on this massage table, but the question could eventually reach the ears of the owner of this establishment.

Jill had irritated her baby sister enough lately.

Noelle Trask ran a tight ship, and she would not take kindly to having her employees verbally abused. Or even questioned by a client with a few…interesting hang-ups. Especially if that client just happened to be her bossy older sister.

Who would have thought Noelle, the wild child of Hideaway High, would have matured so well?

Not Jill. Oh, no. Jill had a tendency to mother Noelle, even though the smart, savvy business woman no longer needed mothering. In fact, she would be a mother herself before long.

Which meant Jill would be an aunt. How she was looking forward to that time—

A sharp jab on her chin startled her. "Ouch!"

"Just relax," Sheena said. "You have a few blemishes here. We can take care of that right—"

"I didn't come here to have my pimples treated, I just want a simple, painless massage." Actually, she hadn't even wanted that.

"Jill Cooper," came a calming voice from another cubicle in the large, cedar-lined spa, "let the lady do her job."

"Yes, Edith," Jill replied, then muttered under her breath, "Noelle needs to get these dividers soundproofed."

"What's that?" Edith Potts called again.

"Nothing. Sorry. I'll be good. I'm having a *simply magnificent* time." Could Edith hear the sarcasm?

"That's my girl."

Nope. Edith had never understood the subtleties of satire. The lady simply said what she thought.

Sheena returned to her massaging. "Will wonders never cease. Edith Potts must be the only person in town you can't boss around."

Jill scowled up at her, and Sheena smiled back, wiggling her perfectly shaped, blond eyebrows.

Eighty-three-year-old Edith Potts, retired principal of Hideaway High, could claim friendship with the majority of Hideaway's residents as well as a few of the flocks of tourists who escaped to this tiny lakeside village every year.

For Jill, Edith epitomized courage. Since Jill often felt as if she, herself, epitomized the exact opposite, she had always been drawn to Edith's independent, nurturing spirit. It was Edith who had found a school nurse position for Jill in Hideaway when tragedy dictated that she would have to return home and be nearby for the family business.

Once again closing her eyes, Jill tried to give herself over to the relaxation Sheena had promised. She had to admit the honey and almond mask smelled heavenly.

Still, if she came away with scars on her face from an over-eager, overly young masseuse, she would hold Edith and Noelle personally responsible. But she wanted a jar of that facial mask, simply for the wonderful fragrance.

In spite of her intentions to remain vigilant, and as if of their own volition, her muscles began to liquefy. She could feel her body merging with the soft sheets and mattress of the massage table until she wasn't sure where the padding ended and her flesh began. What was more, she didn't care.

Jill seldom relaxed. She had often been accused of being one of the most uptight, untouchable single women in Hideaway or the surrounding area. Most of the townsfolk kept such comments out of her earshot—or so they thought—but Edith never hesitated to speak her mind, and neither did Noelle now that she was back in town.

As Jill thought about it, she had recently found herself blessed—if that could be the term for it—by associates at work who never minced words with her.

They understood the term for her condition. Thanks to recent popular television shows, who didn't know what OCD stood for? And yet they wouldn't let her get away with the typical behavior of someone with obsessive-compulsive disorder.

Blessed…yes. That was it. She was truly blessed by people who loved her in spite—

"You could use a good plucking." Sheena's soft voice interrupted Jill's reverie.

"What?" Jill opened her eyes to see the young woman hovering over her, and wielding a pair of tweezers far too close. *Now* what tortures did this over-eager twenty-two-year-old have in mind?

"I want to shape your eyebrows. I can take ten years off your face with a few good yanks."

Jill's liquefied muscles suddenly returned to their original position. "Look, Sheena Marshall," she said, keeping her voice low in deference to Edith, "I didn't come here to be plucked or yanked or tweezed, I just came for a simple massage with this green stuff you smeared all over my face. Now, are you finished?"

"Not yet. There are just so many things you need to have done."

"Shouldn't someone be tending to Edith?"

"She knows how to relax…unlike you."

"Where's your mother? Can't she do the massage?"

"She was only scheduled to work this morning," Sheena sounded a little dejected. "Dad picked her up at noon, and they were going away for the rest of the weekend."

Sheena's mom, Mary Marshall, had agreed to come to work at the spa on an as-needed basis until Noelle knew for sure how many full-time staff members she would require. Not only was Mary an accomplished massage therapist who had worked for years in surrounding resorts, she was also a cosmetologist and had a good head for business. Jill had graduated high school with her.

Sheena still lived at home, and seemed content to stay in Hideaway the rest of her life, living with her parents and working here at the spa. Though Jill had stayed home for several years after graduating from high school, it was out of necessity. Sheena stayed by choice.

What a strange young woman.

Jill shifted on the massage table. "Did I hear Noelle come back from her errands a few minutes ago? Can't she see to Edith while you're doing this massage?"

"We won't be much longer. Noelle warned me not to take too long the first time."

First time? Like this was going to happen again?

Was that laughter she heard in the next room?

Edith had a sense of humor that had brought healing light to some of the darkest moments in Jill's life. Let her laugh.

And yet even as Jill listened to that laughter, it didn't sound quite right.

That wasn't laughter. "Edith, you okay in there? Are you choking?"

For countless seconds there was no answer. Then they heard a loud thunk.

Sudden alarm gripped Jill as she charged up from the massage bed, stumbling against the tray table beside her. Oils and bottles and jars went flying with the movement. She scrambled past Sheena, raced into the hallway and into the next cubicle, her apron billowing around her.

She thrust the door open to find Edith lying on the floor, gnarled hands grasping her throat. Her face was still half-covered with the towel of supposedly soothing herbs. The half that wasn't covered was purple. Her eyes bulged with terror.

"Call for help!" Jill yelled as she dropped to her

knees beside Edith and began wiping the green mask of goo from her face with a towel. "Edith, it's okay. We're going to take care of you."

The lady's mouth worked silently.

"Who do I call?" Sheena cried.

"Get Noelle."

As Sheena skittered from the room, Edith's eyes closed and her body relaxed.

"No, Edith! Don't stop breathing on me! Edith!"

Dear Reader,

Shona Tremaine has had to live with the results of some horrible decisions she has made in her life, which not only affect her but those she loves. She finds that it's impossible to make amends for those decisions, and impossible to forgive herself. It isn't until she opens her heart to God's will in her life that she finds the ability to accept the forgiveness of others, and to allow healing change to take place.

I've found myself in Shona's situation, as you may have been at some time in your life. I believe that sin and failure give Satan an opening in which to wreak havoc upon our relationship with God. He loves to convince us, with thoughts we think belong to us, that God is so disgusted by us, He wants nothing to do with us because of our sin.

We must never forget that the appearance of Jesus Christ here on earth counters that lie. He came for sinners just like us. There is love and forgiveness just waiting for us in His open arms if we will only turn to Him. It's never too late, and we know God causes all things to work together for the good of those who love Him, who are called according to His purpose. Let Him work.

Blessings,

Hannah Alexander

QUESTIONS FOR DISCUSSION

1. *Under Suspicion* is about healing broken relationships. What could Shona have done to prevent those breaks in the first place?

2. Do you think Shona and Karah Lee would have remained friends through the years had their parents never divorced, or would their personalities have still clashed?

3. What could Geoff have done differently in order to protect his marriage from the dilemma he and Shona faced?

4. It is common knowledge that public servants must make a lot of compromises in their positions. What do you feel is acceptable? How far is too far?

5. Kemper MacDonald made a drastic change in his life when he became a Christian. Has your life, or quality of life, ever been threatened because you stood for something in which you believed? Please explain.

6. Shona finds herself mercilessly courted by the press after her father is killed. How much does the public have a right to know about a public servant in Shona's position?

7. Shona and Geoff are both shocked when they discover who Kemper's killer was. Can you tell about a time when you have been deceived or harmed by someone close to you?

8. If someone you loved has hurt you in the past, have you taken steps to forgive that person? How much would it take for you to forgive?

9. If there is someone in your past that you have harmed, have you asked for forgiveness? What led you to do that?

10. Now that Shona and Geoff are reconciled, how will their marriage be different?

2 Love Inspired novels and a mystery gift... Absolutely FREE!

Visit

www.LoveInspiredBooks.com

for your two FREE books, sent directly to you!

BONUS: Choose between regular print or our NEW larger print format!

There's no catch! You're under no obligation to buy anything. We charge nothing—ZERO—for your first shipment. And you don't have to make any minimum number of purchases.

You'll like the convenience of home delivery at our special discount prices, and you'll love your free subscription to Steeple Hill News, our members-only newsletter.

We hope that after receiving your free books, you'll want to remain a subscriber. But the choice is yours—to continue or cancel, anytime at all! So why not take us up on our invitation, with no risk of any kind!

Love Inspired®
SUSPENSE

TITLES AVAILABLE NEXT MONTH

Don't miss these two stories in August

SECRETS OF THE ROSE by Lois Richer
Finders Inc.

After her husband's death, all Shelby Kinkaid had left was her daughter, Aimee, and the business she'd started with her husband. Their agency reunited people with their lost belongings and loved ones. But when Aimee vanished without a trace, Shelby had to rely on a longtime friend to save Aimee's life...and her own.

TANGLED MEMORIES by Marta Perry

For years, teacher Corrie Grant thought she'd never know who her late father was, but when she traveled to Savannah with some new information about his identity, she found the current heirs to her father's family fortune aligned in opposition to her. Lucas Santee was assigned to keep an eye on Corrie, a daunting task when accidents started happening entirely too close to home.

LISCNM0706